Download
Drama

Celeste O. Norfleet

Download Drama

KIMANI
tru
™

Recycling programs
for this product may
not exist in your area.

DOWNLOAD DRAMA

ISBN-13: 978-0-373-53463-0

www.KimaniTRU.com

Printed in U.S.A.

Acknowledgments

Thank you readers, parents, teachers and librarians for recommending and sharing the Kenisha Lewis series. I am truly appreciative.

Writing the stories in the Kenisha Lewis series has been one of my greatest joys. Although her journey to becoming a young woman is filled with struggles and conflicts at nearly every turn, her indomitable spirit continually shines through. She is strong even when she doesn't believe she is. And it is her boundless determination that makes her such a resilient character.

Because of the series, I have met so many wonderful young women, who are inspired by Kenisha's story in their own journey to adulthood. Like Kenisha, they have endured life's challenges, and I applaud their resolve. Circumstances don't define who you are, but rather influence the person you become. Even though you can't always avoid drama, you can overcome it and learn from it. When others say you can't, believe that you can and will succeed, *if* you stay true to yourself.

Please feel free to visit my website, www.celesteonorfleet.wordpress.com, or write me and let me know what you think. I always enjoy hearing from readers. I can be reached at conorfleet@aol.com or Celeste O. Norfleet, P.O. Box 7346, Woodbridge, VA 22195-7346.

Enjoy!

To Fate & Fortune

one

The End of a Not So Good Thing

kenishi_wa K Lewis
Note to self: just breathe
26 Apr * Like * Comment * Share

SO, okay. I finally get it. I'm stuck in Penn Hall's perpetual cycle of BS for the next year and a half. Hazelhurst Academy—the all-girls private school—is in the past and I've reconciled myself to that. So what if Penn is the worst public school in Washington, D.C. I figure it's all about my state of mind. And right now my state of mind is to just suck it up.

If there's one thing I've learned over the past few months, it's that my life is not ordinary. Nothing about it is typical for a sixteen-year-old. My family, my friends, my school and even my shrink, Dr. Tubbs, push my buttons so hard that I'm just a split second away from being in a straitjacket for the rest of my life. My therapist, Dr. Tubbs, has a Freudian fixation, but that's another story for another time.

Of course, this is just my opinion, but right now it happens to be the only opinion that counts. So the question I keep asking myself is this: How did my life get so twisted and how do I straighten it out? Seriously, I don't have a clue.

And I don't think anyone else does, either, so I just keep waiting to see what's gonna happen next.

Right now I don't have a job because of the robbery—more about that later. The girl who I thought was a good friend, it turns out she wasn't. My social life is on lockdown. And my boyfriend, Terrence—well, he's the lawnmower guy—he's cool right now. So what's left? Family? My grandmother's acting like she's a prison warden. My sister thinks she's my bodyguard, and my dad is back to his old ways—sleeping around.

After that there's school, and, well, let's just say it's not exactly something that makes you want to do cartwheels. So now I mostly just text and tweet my real friends—Jalisa and Diamond—and avoid as much drama as possible. LOL. Like that's gonna happen.

I look back at my life sometimes and just shake my head. I wonder why bad things keep happening to me. It's like my life and everything around me is out of control. No matter what I do, drama happens. I blog, I tweet, I text, I talk, I breathe and drama happens. Seriously, all kinds of crazy stuff happens around me. Robberies, break-ins, fights, arguments, crazy dreams, family drama, baby mamma drama, ex-boyfriend drama, new boyfriend drama, new boyfriend's ex-girlfriend drama and that's just in the last few months. I don't know why, but for some reason I'm always in the middle of somebody else's stupid drama. It's like drama has me on speed dial and calls me 24/7. It might sound strange to some. But believe me, it's the norm for me.

But that was then. For the first time in a really long time, I, Kenisha Lewis, am having ordinary, boring, drama-free days. For real! Trust me, if you knew my life you'd know that doesn't happen very often. So when it does, hell, yeah,

I'm worried. Most people would be ecstatic about it. But like I said, my life is drama-free now. I'm on a roll and I don't want to chance screwing it up.

I get out my cell and hit up Twitter.

kenishi_wa K Lewis
i finished my chemistry exam early—it was 2 easy. now im just sitn n class waiting...bored... 10 minutes ago

kenishi_wa K Lewis
still waiting & still bored—i have 2 more classes to go but im so ready to get out of here now. 2 minutes ago

My cell vibrates.

jalisa_jas Jalisa Saunders
@kenishi_wa *i kno that's tru. im n humanities right now. we r reading metamorphosis—gross. bored... sleepy. i want 2 go home 2 bed.* 2 minutes ago

diamond_jewels Diamond Riggs
@kenishi_wa *ditto for me. im in advanced algebra. tired of numbers, equations and formulas. i just want to go home & sleep.* 2 minutes ago

kenishi_wa K Lewis
lol—we gotta stop talking & texting all night.
1 minute ago

jalisa_jas Jalisa Saunders
@kenishi_wa *can u c us not talking and texting all night?* 1 minute ago

diamond_jewels Diamond Riggs
@kenishi_wa *nope. not really. 2 much 2 talk about.*
1 minute ago

kenishi_wa K Lewis
you mean 2 many people 2 talk about—lol.
1 minute ago

jalisa_jas Jalisa Saunders
@kenishi_wa *lol & smh.* 1 minute ago

kenishi_wa K Lewis
5...4...3...2...1 OUTTA HERE! LATER! 25 seconds ago

The bell rings, signaling that it's time for fifth-period classes, but I already decided not to go. I'm not in the mood to listen to Mr. Wells lecture us about computer stuff I already know. My dad owns a computer company, so basically everything he teaches is redundant. I know this stuff. Word processing, Photoshop, Flash, Dreamweaver—I played with those when I was in elementary school. So skipping his class is no big deal. It's not like I'm gonna miss anything. Plus, I just found out that Ms. Grayson, my history teacher, is out today and we have a substitute. That means watching a stupid movie for fifty minutes. Yep, I'm skipping that class, too.

I go to my locker, get my jacket and my backpack and then head to the exit doors. There are a lot of other students leaving, too. They're mostly seniors with lighter class schedules, so I just blend in with them. Nobody asks where I'm going, not even the aide standing by the door, so I just keep walking like I'm supposed to be leaving. She looks at me but doesn't say a word.

As soon as I step outside I feel it—freedom. There's nothing like it. And in another thirty-two hours I'm gonna be completely liberated. My grandmother's going to Georgia to visit her sister. She'll be gone for the next week. She planned it way before my mom died and before I came to live with her. She was gonna cancel the trip, especially after everything that happened. But I convinced her to go. Seriously, she needed a break.

I zip my jacket up and adjust my hoodie as a chilly breeze cuts through me. I hate this time of year. It's cold and wet and miserable one day, then warm and nice the next. It's been raining off and on for the past three days and the sky is a cloudy gray. The ground is wet and there are puddles in potholes everywhere. I start walking across the parking lot. As soon as I get to the other side, it starts to drizzle. Usually, I don't mind when the weather changes, but today I do. My hands are cold, so I pull my gloves on, take my iPhone out and plug in my earbuds to listen to my music.

A few seconds into my song I get a phone call. I check the caller ID. It's my dad. I don't know why he's calling me now. He knows I'm supposed to be in class. But since I don't want to be bothered, I just ignore the call and let it go to voice mail. I really don't feel like dealing with him.

It takes about ten minutes to walk home. Well, it's not actually home for real. It's my grandmother's house in northwest D.C. I walk down the empty street and hurry up the front steps to the porch. As soon as I open the door, I know my grandmother is away. Perfect. I disengage the new alarm system we had installed a few weeks ago, then reset it since I'm here alone. I go up to my room, quickly change my clothes and put on my belly shirt, leotards and baggy dance sweats. I grab a couple of bottles of water from the refrigerator and write a note for my grandmother. I've been thinking about this all day. The music's in my head and I can't wait to get started.

Dancing is the one thing that I really love. I'm good at it, really good. When I dance, I feel like I own the world. I have no fears, no doubts and no reservations. It's just me and the music. It doesn't matter what kind of dance I do 'cause I love them all—jazz, ballet, modern, calypso, tap and especially hip-hop. There's something about just letting the music move your body that frees your mind of everything. When I dance I don't worry about money, or family or boyfriends. All that just fades away. And the only place to dance is at Freeman Dance Studio.

I pick up my bag and lock the front door behind me. I step outside my grandmother's house, stand on the porch and look up and down the street. It's still early afternoon, so most of the neighbors are at work. I start walking down the steps and notice just how peaceful it is. I don't mean just the neighborhood, although that's quiet, too, but my life is quiet.

As soon as I reach the sidewalk, I see Cassie Mosley walking down the street with two other girls—ninth graders. I've seen them at school and around the way. I don't know them, but I do know Cassie—all too well. She's a straight-up hater with major issues, and that's a dangerous combination. I don't even look her way. She's not worth it. But I know she's watching me. She's always mugging me behind my back. It used to bother me, but now I really don't care. I just ignore her and continue down the front steps and head in the direction of Freeman. I get halfway down the block when I hear my name. "Yo, Kenisha," someone yells.

Damn. Of course I know who it is. I turn around and see Li'l T running down the street to catch up with me. I don't know why, but we've kinda connected lately. Well, maybe not really connected. He's still the biggest gossip in the neighborhood. And he still gets on my nerves sometimes, but not as much as he used to. He's like a younger brother that's always following me around driving me crazy. Still, I really don't feel like dealing with him and hearing about everybody's drama. But I slow down a second or two, anyway. It's not that Li'l T is bad or anything, he just takes a lot of getting used to.

"You cutting class?" he says as soon as he reaches me.

"No, I'm maximizing my available time," I say.

"Yeah, right, that's called cutting." He laughs.

"So what are *you* doing out of school?" I ask.

"I had a doctor's appointment," he says. "So where are you going?"

"To Freeman," I say.

"You gonna dance?"

"Yes," I say.

"Yo, can I watch?"

"No."

"See you wrong, you know that. But that's cool, that's a'ight. So check it out," he says, showing me his new iPad. "I just got it. It's tight, right."

"Yeah, I've seen these. They're nice," I say nonchalantly, because I've seen a couple dozen computer tablets before. My dad has them at his job.

"Nah, nah, nah, you ain't seen this one—not yet, anyway."

I check out the front and see that it's not what I thought it was. He taps the screen and turns it on. The screen instantly lights up. It looks like it's already loaded with every app program imaginable. "Wait, that's the new version," I say in a surprised voice since I know this version isn't supposed to be released for another eight months, at least. My dad has a computer company, so I usually get stuff early, but never this early. "This isn't even out yet. How'd you get it already?"

"My cousin Bo got it for me."

I look at him like I know better 'cause I do. "Stuff like this falls off the back of a truck all the time, but not this time. Nah, these can't fall off a truck since they're not even supposed to be on a truck yet."

"For real, it's legit. He's got the serious hookup. Check it out. This baby is fully loaded, too. It does everything, even video and editing. It's like a mini movie studio, just point and shoot. Then there's this app that I can upload and send video directly to YouTube and Facebook. So you know I'm gonna rock this baby to start my new business," he adds excitedly.

I look at him skeptically. "Your new business," I repeat. "It sounds like more trouble to me. You better be careful."

"Nah, I got this all figured out. See, whenever something jumps off I'm gonna film it. You know I'm gonna be a filmmaker, right."

"Really," I say halfheartedly 'cause every week he changes his career to something different. "Wait, didn't you tell me last week you're gonna be a record producer and the week before that a rapper. So what happened to all that?"

"It's all the same thing. It's called talent. That's what I got."

"Right, talent," I say, mildly amused. I notice that he's got this big bruise and a puffy eye. "What's up with your face?"

"What? Nothing," he says dismissively.

"Don't tell me you got in trouble and got your butt kicked," I say. Then I see his expression changes like he's scared or something. He turns his head and looks in the other direction. I stop walking and pull his arm toward me to stop him. "What happened?" I ask. He doesn't say anything. I know right then I'm right. Somebody beat him up. I also know he's not gonna tell me who did it. Snitches get stitches. "Are you okay?" I ask quietly.

"Girl, I'm fine. Like I said, it's nothing. I was just messing around."

He starts walking. I follow this time. Neither one of us says anything for a while. Then we walk past Darien's house just as he comes out on the front porch. I haven't seen him in months and now he just walks out like he owns the neighborhood. He glares at us hard like he's about to say something, but he doesn't. He just looks. I look, too. I can't believe he's here.

"I thought he was gone for good. What's he doing back here?" I ask under my breath.

"Didn't you hear? He got off on a technicality. Something about what the cops did when they arrested him for the attempted robbery at your grandmother's house. Now they're saying they didn't have probable cause to search the house the night of the fight, so that's probably gonna be thrown out, too."

"That's crazy."

"Yeah, well, you know he's getting off on that charge, too. Stuff always happens like that. I swear, it must be nice doing whatever you want and getting away with it all the time because your father just about runs city hall."

We walk past him and I hear his cell phone ringing. I turn around and see that he's still staring at us—no, he's staring at me. Then he smiles, and I look away. "I really hate that guy."

"He's just a punk-ass bully," Li'l T says way too loud. "He's got all these people protecting him and he never gets in trouble. He killed T's little brother, then he goes up on drug possession charges and breaking into your house and still nothing happens to him. The legal system is bullshit. All you gotta do is know someone like his dad does."

"That's how it always is," I say.

"Well, somebody needs to change things. You know his dad wants to run for mayor of D.C., right. I hear that's why they shipped his ass back here. Can you imagine what he's gonna be like if his dad is mayor?"

I look at Li'l T. Suddenly there's something different about him. It's the first time I've ever heard him talk like this. I've seen Li'l T angry, pissed, scared, happy and excited, but I've never seen him like this before.

"Is he the one who messed up your face?" I ask him.

"No," he says quickly.

I don't know why, but I believe him. But I also think he got a beat-down. I just wish he'd trust me enough to tell me who did it.

When we get to Freeman, he stops and looks around. "You must be a really good dancer by now. You come to this place almost every day."

"Yeah, I'm pretty good."

"So you gonna show me your moves so I can video you?"

"Hell, no," I say jokingly. We laugh as I head up the steps and he keeps walking. "See you later. Be careful," I say.

I watch as he waves without turning around and just keeps walking. When he gets to the corner I open the door and go inside. Everything suddenly changes. I enter the studio like I own it. It's my place, my home. I don't actually have a dance class today. And I usually don't come to the studio until the end of the week, but today I just feel like dancing.

TWO

Dancing Free

kenishi_wa K Lewis
I'm happy. I love my life. Everything is perfect, or as close to perfect as it can be. All I want to do is dance. I hear the music. I feel the movements. I dance.
26 Apr * Like * Comment * Share

AS soon as I enter the building I smile. I can feel it all around me—a sense of levity, lightness. It's like I'm weightless, floating, and all my burdens have been lifted. I know the history of the place, but it's more than that. It's about feeling free. No wonder they named the place Freeman. It's like breathing fresh air. It fills my lungs and renews me.

I head down the hall to the main office. As I walk through the corridor, I see pictures of me and my girls on the wall. I smile proudly. It feels good to know that no matter what happens in my life I can always come back to Freeman. The office door is open and I see Ms. Jay, the director, sitting at her desk on the computer. "Hi, Ms. Jay," I say, poking my head into her office as I stand beside the doorway.

She looks up, smiling. "Hi, Kenisha," she says, then

checks her watch and frowns. "What are you doing here this early? Shouldn't you still be in school?"

"We have a substitute so I didn't have to go to my last class." Okay, so it's not exactly the whole truth, but it's close enough. "Can I use one of the private studios upstairs?"

"Oh, unfortunately, there's a problem with the upstairs rooms."

"What's the problem?" I ask.

"After it rained the past few nights, the roof started leaking again. The rooms are still flooded. It's the fifth time this year. This time the wood floor in Studio A buckled in a few places and the other two studios still have water leaking from the roof. There are buckets everywhere."

"Oh, no," I say, disappointed. I was really looking forward to dancing today. I have the perfect ending for my routine. And as soon as I put it together I'm gonna show my girls. So I really need to practice. "How long do you think it's gonna take to fix?"

She shakes her head slowly. "To tell you the truth, Kenisha, I don't know if I'll be able to fix it this time. We need a new roof and about a hundred other repairs around here." She pauses. "I just don't have the money to fix everything. As a matter of fact, I'm thinking about making some changes."

"What kind of changes?"

"Closing down the studio," she says.

"You mean moving the studio someplace else?" I ask.

"No, I mean closing it down for good." She shakes her head again. "It's too much and sometimes it's just not worth it."

As soon as she says those words, I swear my jaw drops and my heart stops beating. Closing the dance studio would be like losing my best friend. "Ms. Jay, you can't do that," I say, walking over to her desk. "There are so many kids who depend on this studio. And it's not just about dance. It's about coming here and being together with friends. You can't close it down."

"I'm sorry, Kenisha, but I don't think I'm going to have much of a choice. Running this place is expensive and I don't see a lot of money coming in anytime soon. But none of this is your problem. Here, take this," she says as she reaches into her desk drawer and pulls out a set of keys. "You can use the auditorium stage today. The light panel is just inside the door on the right-hand side. This key unlocks the sound system cabinet backstage. If you have an iPhone or an iPod you can plug it in. Thankfully the sound system is the one thing still working around here."

"Thank you," I say, taking the keys and walking toward the door. "How much money do you think you'll need to fix everything?"

"A lot," she says. "Do me a favor. I don't want a whole bunch of kids hanging out in the auditorium."

"They won't. It'll just be me. I promise."

"All right, and make sure to lock the music cabinet when you're finished. I'd hate to have another sound system stolen."

"I'll definitely make sure to lock the cabinet, I promise. Thanks again, Ms. Jay." I turn to leave, then turn around again. "Ms. Jay, what about doing a fundraiser to get the money."

"What do you mean?"

"I mean, like one of those talent shows on TV where you can have judges and contestants and a prize. You can charge people to come and watch. I can help and I'm sure Jalisa and Diamond would want to help, too. You can maybe get Tyrece and Gayle Harmon to judge if they're around."

Ms. Jay nods and looks like she might be interested. "You know, that's not a bad idea. I'll think about it."

I turn around and head toward the auditorium, which is right down the hall. All of the sudden I get a knot in my stomach. I can't believe Ms. Jay is even considering closing the studio. This is where I grew up. I met my two best friends here. I don't know what I'd do without this place.

I open the auditorium doors. It's dark and quiet inside, like a scene out of a horror movie. I look around, but it's too dark to really see anything. I feel for the light panel, then start flipping switches. All the lights turn on, instantly illuminating the large cavernous space in a soft glow. When I hit the last switch the stage lights flick on. I decide to turn the rest of the lights off and just leave the stage illuminated.

I start walking toward the stage. It's creepy at first. I've never been alone in here before. But then I kinda like the solitude. It's quiet. All I can hear are my footsteps and there's nothing around me except for the wooden flip-down theater seats in rows arcing around the stage.

I climb the five steps to the stage, step into the single spotlight, then turn around and look back toward the seats. At first there's nothing but darkness, then my eyes adjust to the brightness. I remember having my recitals here on this stage. I would dance and my mom would be in the audience clapping and calling out my name. I smile, thinking about the last recital I had. It was years ago, but I remember it like it was yesterday. I performed a ballet solo. I was good. Afterward my mom was so proud she cried all the way home to Virginia. She had no idea I was as talented as I was.

The curtains are open so I head backstage. I take off my jacket and change into my dance shoes. I unlock the cabinet for the sound system and place my iPhone in the docking station and press Play. The music starts playing through the speaker system. I start stretching as the music plays. Fifteen minutes later a Ty Grant song comes on and I do a dance routine. When it goes off, I go backstage and put my musical playlist on a continuous loop. I walk to center stage. As soon as the music starts, I begin hip-hop dancing.

The rhythm of the beat takes over and all of the sudden I lose control. My body becomes one with the music. It's not me dancing. It's the music flowing through my body making me move. The pulsating beat surrounds me and I let the music take over.

Locking, popping, freestyle, old-school L.A. krumping—the combinations flow one right after the other. The movements are fluid and in perfect sync with the music. My facial expressions stay on point and my choreography is perfect.

It's my own arrangement. I used my keyboard at home to create the music and rhythms. I mixed the beat and added the melody with other instruments. Then I downloaded the whole thing on to my computer and, using software, I remixed the tracks until they sounded incredible. I found a poem in my recipe book and added the lyrics. I rapped and then added a gritty vocal track to the chorus. I have to admit, it's really pretty good. When I played it for my girls they loved it. Then the more I listened to it the more I saw the choreography play out in my head—part ballet, jazz and a lot of hip-hop.

I start practicing, focusing on control and execution. I keep going over and over it again. Each time I do it I can feel it getting better and better. My body loosens up and the movements flow. At the end of the track, I move my hips and lock my arms and do the turn. The dance feels good. I start smiling. This is exactly like I want it. The music loops a few more times and soon the choreography is perfect. I practice the routine one more time, and as the music stops I hold the end stance longer. I close my eyes and smile. *Perfect*.

"Booya!"

I open my eyes quickly and look around. Someone is in the back of the auditorium applauding like crazy. At first I can't tell who it is because the stage lights are really bright. Then I recognize the voice. "Now that's what's up. Yo, yo, yo, girl, that was the shit. I'm talking BET, MTV, VH1 combined. They ain't got nothin' on you. Yeah, that's what's up—for real."

I squint into the darkened theater and see Li'l T sitting in one of the back rows with his feet propped up on the seat in front of him. He jumps up and continues applauding and whistling. "Li'l T, what are you doing in here?" I ask breathlessly.

"Checking you out, girl, you was awesome. You should seriously be dancing professionally. That was tight."

"Yeah, whatever... Look you need to get out of here."

"See, I'm paying you a compliment and you actin' all cold. But check, whose rap is that?"

"It's mine."

"Seriously? For real? That's your work?" he asks.

I nod and pick up a bottle of water, practically downing it in one gulp. "Damn, girl, I didn't know you rolled like that. I'm impressed, you got serious talent. You did the music and the lyrics."

"Yeah, what do you think?"

"I think you need to market that. Nah, forget that. You need to let me produce and put you out there. Yeah, people do it all the time. Look at Taj, she got discovered on the YouTube doing exactly what you just did and she ain't half as good as you."

I start laughing. He steps into the aisle and gets real serious as he moves closer to the stage. "Nah, nah, nah, for real… Listen, check it out. I can video you dancing. I'll edit it, and then put you up on YouTube, and in a week I bet you you'll be famous just like Taj."

"Yeah, right, you do that," I say sarcastically. "You gotta get out. I told Ms. Jay I'd be the only one in here."

"Yeah, yeah… A'ight. I hear you," he says as he starts walking backward up the aisle to the doors. "But check, you gonna be famous when I'm done."

"Yeah, whatever," I shout out to him as I head back to the stage again.

"A'ight, later."

As soon as I hear the door close I press a few buttons on my iPhone and replay the music again. I sit down on the stage and just listen this time. I start smiling to myself. He's right, it is good. After a while I change out of my dance shoes and put on my toe shoes. I flex my feet several times to loosen up, then spend a few more minutes stretching the leg muscles I'll need to practice another routine.

I go backstage to change the music and put on something that me and my girls have been working on for a while. The music plays and I do a series of spins and hit my mark at center stage. I stop on the same beat as the music, then I get into position two and elevate on my toes. The movement is flawless. I begin to dance and continue blending one routine into another. Then after a while my legs start to tighten up. That happens when I do ballet, and then I know it's time to stop.

The music slows and I stop dancing and bow gracefully, then look out at the empty seats. I imagine the applause and smile to myself. But really all I see are the spotlights on the stage and the darkness beyond it. Then out of the darkness I see the silhouette of someone sitting in the back row. They start clapping. "Li'l T," I yell out. No one answers. I know it's Li'l T again. I break position and put my fists on my hips and call out to him. "Boy, if you don't get out of here I'm gonna kick your butt." He still doesn't say anything. Then I see him get up and walk out. But I know from the shadowy outline it's not Li'l T. I have no idea who it is.

three

Starting Something New

kenishi_wa K Lewis
I can hear them coming. The footsteps are getting closer and closer. Pretty soon everything behind me will catch up with everything in front of me.
26 Apr * Like * Comment * Share

I don't dance in front of audiences anymore, so knowing that someone was watching me just now feels weird. And not knowing who it was is creepy. They just got up and left. You see, dancing is personal for me. I don't mind dancing in front of people. I've been doing it all my life. But I only dance for an audience when I know the performance is the best it can be. So having someone sneak in uninvited and see me practicing is wrong. I stand center stage a few minutes longer wondering if whoever it was is gonna have the nerve to come back again. After a while I realize they don't.

I look around and notice I'm just standing in an empty auditorium looking at nothing. All of the sudden being here doesn't seem like a good idea anymore. I turn to go back-stage. I grab my cell phone off the dock, lock up the sound system and then pick up my jacket and grab my dance bag.

It's time to leave. As I walk out the auditorium I check my cell phone messages. I have six text messages and three missed calls, one from my grandmother, one from my dad and one from my sister. I call my grandmother back first 'cause I know she's been really stressing about me lately.

I really wish she'd just chill, but I don't see that happening anytime soon. I know it's all because of the drama I had a few weeks ago at the house and at the pizza place. Neither break-in was my fault, but it still seems like I'm being punished because a couple of idiots acted like fools. I get that she loves me and she worries. But now she wants me to check in and let her know everywhere I go all the time. It's driving me crazy.

Even though she never says it, I feel like I'm on lockdown. And it's not just her. My sister acts the same way, too, like I'm gonna all of the sudden get struck by lightning or something. The thing is I know anything can happen to anybody at any time and it usually does, especially around me. I guess I have bad luck or maybe no luck at all.

The studio seems as quiet and just as empty as it was before. There are only a few students walking around. I guess not a lot of kids take dance class during the week anymore. It's strange because when I took classes this place was teeming with students.

The phone rings, like, four times. Now I start wondering what's taking my grandmother so long to answer the phone. On the next ring she finally picks up. When she says hello I can hear that she's out of breath. "Hi, Grandmom, it's me. Is everything okay?" I ask.

"Hi, sweetheart, yes, everything's fine. I was out on the front porch and forgot to take the cordless with me. I had to come back inside the house to answer. I called you almost an hour ago. Are you just getting the message?"

"Yes. I was dancing and my cell was turned off," I say, hoping this isn't going to turn into another one of her lectures about always keeping in touch. I get those a lot lately.

"Where are you?" she asks.

"I'm at Freeman. I came here right after school. I left you a note on the kitchen table. Didn't you get it?"

"Yes, I got it. How was school?"

"It was okay. We had a substitute."

"Do you have homework?"

"No. I just have to read and I can do that tonight."

"All right. It'll be dark soon, so don't stay out too late. You still have school tomorrow."

"I know. I won't be long," I say, ready to hang up, anticipating her lecture. But I'm just not in the mood today.

"You know you have to be extra careful now because…"

Too late, she starts. "I know, Grandmom, I know," I say, but she keeps going, anyway.

"…that Darien Moore is back on the streets again. I don't know what it's going to take for the police to put him behind bars and keep him there for good. He's a menace to this neighborhood and to the…"

There's no stopping her now. So I just lean back, tune out and wait until she's finished. It's not like she's wrong. She's not. It's true. Darien gets in trouble, gets locked up and then gets out a week later. It's crazy, like a revolving door.

"…and the streets are getting worse and worse. People don't respect anything, least of all one another. They don't care about the consequences of their actions. Young doesn't mean immortal…"

"I know, Grandmom, I know. Wait, did you already go to bingo tonight?" I ask, knowing that she didn't and that it starts in an hour. That's just an attempt to interrupt the lecture. Then I tell her that I see my dance instructor coming down the hallway for class. It's not a lie. I do see my instructor, but she was my dance teacher when I was ten years old.

"Okay, you go ahead to class. Remember, don't stay too late."

"I know. Have fun at bingo," I say as I wave to my old ballet teacher as she passes me in the hallway and heads to one of the dance studios followed by a few pint-size ballet students in leotards, tights and slippers. I remember being that age and wanting to be a ballerina. I shake my head and smile just as another call beeps. I look at the small screen. It's my dad. "Grandmom, Dad's calling on the other line."

"Okay. Talk to him. He's worried. He called here earlier looking for you. Apparently, you had an appointment with Dr. Tubbs today and missed it without calling."

"Oh, I forgot all about my appointment today. I came right here after school."

"You speak with your dad and don't stay out too late."

"Okay, see you later, Grandmom." She hangs up. I let my dad's call go to voice mail. Since I already know what he wants, I decide to catch up with him later. The last thing I want to hear is him complaining about paying for my therapist. Still, I can't believe I missed my appointment with Dr. Tubbs. I've been seeing him for a few months now. And even though I thought I wouldn't, I really like talking to him. He's ancient and I'm sure has no idea what I'm talking about sometimes. But all in all, he's pretty cool for an old guy. After a few minutes I call my sister.

Jade picks up on the second ring. "Hey," she says.

"Hey, girl, what's up?"

"Where are you?" she asks.

"I'm at Freeman. I left school early and came here to dance."

"You mean you cut class?" she clarifies.

"Trust me, it's no big deal. One was a computer class and I already so know more than what's being taught and the other was Ms. Grayson's class. She was out today. We had a substitute and I wasn't in the mood to watch a Disney movie so I left."

"I found out about the hospital bills."

"What about them?" I ask.

"They're not Grandmom's. They belong to mom."

"What? When was she in the hospital?"

"I don't know yet, but we need to get together and talk. Are you going to your dad's house in Virginia this weekend?"

"I can stay here," I say.

"Good, okay. I'll meet you tomorrow after school."

"Okay, call me." I end the call and just stand there with a blank expression on my face. Now I'm even more confused than I was before. How did my mom have thousands of dollars in hospital bills and no one knew about it? All of a sudden I feel like I need to get home quick. But there's nothing I can do when I get there, anyway. Talk about feeling helpless.

I grab my bag and head back to the main office to return the key to Ms. Jay.

When I get to the office I see Ms. Jay on the phone. She looks upset. I think she's talking to one of her teachers. I wave and mouth the words *thank you*. She nods as she takes the key and puts it back in her desk drawer.

I head toward the front door to go home, but then I spy Ursula coming toward the office. She doesn't see me because she's laughing and talking with some other girls. I stop and take a step back. We haven't really been close since her half brother, Darien, broke into my house. She called me a couple of times, but I just texted her back that I couldn't talk.

The truth is I don't really want to talk to her right now. I have some things to figure out. I'm not blaming her for Darien and his stupid drama. I know she has nothing to do with him and that she hates him as much as I do, maybe even more. But he wasn't alone in my house when he broke in. I know I heard a girl's voice that night. I just wish I knew who it was.

I like Ursula. She's a good friend. She's fun and she's real. She says what she thinks and doesn't care how it comes out. She's like my two best friends, Jalisa and Diamond, mixed together. But now I keep thinking, what if it was her that night? And then I start wondering, what if she was really with Darien and Cassie when they tried to set me up? I don't want to accuse her, because if I'm wrong...

I'd hate to lose her as a friend. That's why I didn't tell anybody what I heard since I'm really not sure. It sounded like Ursula in my house the night of the robbery, but I don't know. Either way, I don't want to deal with it. I turn around and head in the other direction.

Since I know the top-floor studios were flooded, I decide to go to one of the smaller studios on the second floor. The rooms are mostly for intermediate students and there's a class just ending, so I go in and sit in the back of the room.

Hopefully there's no dance class in here now. I could seriously use some peace and quiet. I pull out my recipe book. But before I start writing, I text Jalisa and Diamond back and leave a message on my dad's office phone. I know he's not there, but at least I can say I called him back.

"Hey, Kenisha," Ursula calls as she walks into the studio.

I look up and see her coming toward me. She's smiling like nothing's happened. But maybe nothing did happen. I really don't know. It could have been her voice and then again… Either way, I smile and assume she's my friend for now.

"Hey," I say, "what are you doing here?"

"I'm taking a hip-hop dance class," she says.

"For real," I say, surprised.

"Yeah, girl, you, Diamond and Jalisa were so great when I saw you dancing before that I decided to try it, too. I'm nowhere near as good as you guys, but I really like it. The instructors are fierce here. I never knew they were so good. A couple of them even danced professionally with the Alvin Ailey company. Can you believe it?"

"Yeah, I know, and this is where Gayle Harmon started."

"I know, that's so cool," she says excitedly. "So what are you doing in here? Do you have class?"

"Nah, I'm just hanging out."

"Waiting for your girls?"

"Nah, we don't usually get together until the weekend. Today I just felt like dancing, so I skipped my last period and came here."

"Seriously, if I danced like you, I wouldn't even go to school anymore. I'd get a job dancing professionally and start making some big bank."

I shake my head. "Nah, not my thing," I say as I watch

more students come in. They're loud and rowdy. Ursula waves at a few girls in the class, but continues talking to me.

"I gotta tell you something," she says softly.

"About Darien," I say.

She nods.

"Yeah, I saw him today."

"His dad dropped him off last night. I hate it," she says, looking away and shaking her head. "We always get stuck with him at the house. His dad gets him out and we have to deal with him. I swear my mom is so pathetic. Whenever his dad says do, she does. You know she still loves him even though he has a wife and family. They even hang out sometimes. It's so pathetic. Somebody should really get rid of Darien permanently."

I look at her strange 'cause it's the same thing Li'L T said, although I don't tell her. A few seconds later the teacher comes in. The music starts and she tells everybody to start stretching. "I guess I'd better get out of here." I stand up and grab my things. "I'll see you later."

"Okay, later. Wait, what are you doing this weekend? My cousin is having a party."

"T's supposed to come home, so we're probably gonna hang out together," I say. She nods. "I'll see you later." She nods again, then looks away and starts stretching. I leave feeling kind of bad now. I didn't exactly lie to Ursula, but I didn't exactly tell her the truth, either. My boyfriend, Terrence, did say he might be coming home this weekend so we can hang out. But he said that last weekend, too, and he never came.

I know he's busy with college courses and his job. But ever since his old girlfriend, Gia, returned, I don't see him as much. He says there's nothing between them, but that's what he thinks. What Gia thinks is something altogether different.

I head back downstairs. Just as I get to the front door and reach for the handle, I hear my name called. I turn around and see Ms. Jay rushing toward me. "Kenisha, I'm glad I caught you. Do you have a few minutes?"

"Sure," I say.

"Come into the office. I'd like to speak to you."

Okay, now my stomach jumps. I know anytime someone wants to talk to me, there's trouble. I know I locked the sound system in the auditorium. I think. Crap, did I?

As soon as I get to her office she turns around to look at me without saying a word. She's just staring at me like she's assessing me. "Um, thanks again, Ms. Jay, for letting me practice in the auditorium," I say, starting to feel uncomfortable.

"No problem," she says, then walks over and sits on the side of her desk. "I need a huge favor and I'm hoping you can help me with this. Do you have any plans this evening?"

"No, not really," I say. "I was just on my way home, that's all."

"Okay, two of my instructors called in sick and another one is going to be a half hour late. I'm going to combine beginning and intermediate ballet and teach that class, but that still leaves me with another class without an instructor. It's the beginning hip-hop class and I really don't want to cancel it. The students in the class are mostly in middle school. Do you think you can take that class for me? You don't really have to teach them any moves, just talk to them about your experience here at the school and maybe show them a few of your earlier hip-hop routines. Also, there might be a few parents looking in. Do you think you can handle that?"

"Can I use my own music?" I ask.

"Sure, as long as it's appropriate."

"It is," I say quickly. Actually, it's no big deal. It's just showing the class a few steps.

She nods. "Great, thank you. I'll go in, introduce you and get you started." She grabs a small portable sound system and I follow her to the second floor to the studio next to where Ursula is taking class. We walk in and there're about fifteen middle school students already there. They start checking me out.

Some of them I've seen before and they kinda know me from the neighborhood. Ms. Jay introduces me as one of her star dance students. She also says some other stuff about my dancing skills and my connection to Gayle Harmon, the choreographer. The kids start looking at me. Some look impressed and some don't. Ms. Jay tells them to start stretching, then looks at me, nods and leaves. Okay, now all of the sudden I'm not as confident as I was in her office, but I know I have to do something.

I stand there a few seconds and then pull my cell phone out of my bag and place it on the portable speaker dock. My music starts playing and I start feeling it. I tell the class to spread out. I show them a few basic hip-hop moves. They're easy, so most of them pick them up pretty fast. I keep adding on to the first part, then about fifteen minutes into the class I get comfortable and start to relax. We practice dancing for a while longer, then I divide them into two groups for a dance-off.

I show them what to do and how to do it, then encourage them to improvise from what I've taught them. They start dancing and I can't believe how good they are. By the time the class is over we're all dancing, joking, laughing and having a great time. I end the class by putting on my ballet slippers and doing what I call hip-hop ballet. They're awed and I love it. When the class is over a few of the parents hang around to talk to me about my teaching. They basically tell me how impressed they are with my dancing. When they leave I take off my ballet shoes, get my cell phone and grab the music system and head out.

As soon as I get outside the class I see this young girl sitting alone on the floor beside the door. She was in my class, but she wasn't all that good. "Hi," I say. She looks up at me. I already see attitude in her eyes. She looks pissed and doesn't speak. She's got her earbuds in her ears, listening to music. "Are you waiting for someone?" I ask louder.

"Yeah," she says louder because of the music.

"Your mom?"

"No, my brother, my half brother."

"Does he know where to find you?"

"He'd better," she says with way too much attitude.

"Maybe he's downstairs waiting for you," I say.

"He said to wait up here."

"What's your name?" I ask her.

"Hannah."

"I'm Kenisha. So are you taking any other dance classes, Hannah?"

"Yeah, I had a ballet class earlier."

"Ballet and hip-hop are my favorites. Do you like them?"

"No, not really," she says drily, "but I don't have a choice. I have to take them."

"How old are you?"

"Ten."

"That's a good age. I started dance class here when I was four years old. My girls and I have been coming here ever since."

She actually turns and looks at me. "Four years old? I can't imagine you dancing at four."

"Well, I wasn't all that good at it then. But I kept practicing and kept getting better. Look, I'll show you a picture of me, come here," I say. She stands up and we walk down the hall to the photos on the wall just outside one of the classrooms. My picture is still hanging there. I show her.

She laughs, then looks at me. "You look funny."

I'm just about to respond when I hear that name I hate. "Check out Kenishiwa."

I stop cold. Only one person still calls me that—Troy Carson. I turn around and see him walking down the hallway smiling. "So you teach, too, huh," he adds.

"Troy, what are you doing here?"

He smiles. "I saw you dancing."

I was a little surprised. I didn't see him in the dance studio, but I was too focused on teaching and dancing to notice the people sitting and standing in the back of the room watching us. "What are you doing here?" I ask him again.

"Picking up my little sister—she goes here now." He playfully pulls an earbud out of Hannah's ear and she pushes his hand away.

I look at her. She rolls her eyes and pokes her lips out. But I can tell she doesn't mean it. It's the same way I pretend with my two little brothers. Then I see the family resemblance. They look a lot alike.

When he walks up he turns to see what we were looking at. "Whoa, check you out. That's you? How old were you?"

"I was four years old."

"No wonder you look so good up there dancing."

"Careful," I warn. "That almost sounds like a compliment. We wouldn't want that. It would mess up your perfect record."

"It was a compliment," he says softly. "You look really good up there."

I look at him strange, then look away. He smiles and I almost believe him—almost. "I saw you and your girls dancing one time. Y'all look really good, like professional dancers."

I shake my head. "We're usually just trying out new moves. We keep changing the routine. As soon as we get it perfect we're gonna show Gayle Harmon and Ty."

"That's right, you roll like that. You know Tyrece Grant."

"You know Tyrece Grant?" his sister asks excitedly.

I nod, looking at her instead of him. "Yeah, he's a good friend of my sister's. We all hang out when he's in town."

"You mean like his entourage."

"No, he's not really like what you see on television and read about in the gossip sites. It's all just image. He acts all hard, but he's a really nice guy."

"Is that what you like?" Troy asks.

"What do you mean?" I ask.

"Nice guys. Is that what you like?"

I'm no fool. I get what he's saying. I know where this is going. But I can't go there, not with him. "Yeah, I do. The guy I'm hanging with now is a nice guy."

He smiles and nods kinda like he's about to challenge me. "Yeah, I heard. You and Terrence, right."

"Yeah, that's right."

"How's that working out for you?"

"He's at Howard and I'm here. We get together when we can," I say. He nods like he hears me, but really none of that seems to faze him. He keeps looking at me, and believe me, I know that look. "Well, I gotta go. See you later."

"Yeah, later," he says as his sister hurries back down the hall to get her dance bag.

I quickly go downstairs to the office to drop off the iPod speaker system. It's getting late and I know I have to get home now. "All done," I say when I see Ms. Jay in her office.

"Did you have a good time?" she asks.

"Oh, my God, Ms. Jay, that was great. I can't believe how much fun it was and they were really good, too."

"Actually, I hear you were just as good. As a matter of fact, quite a few of the parents mentioned they were really impressed with the way you taught the dance class."

"Really," I say happily.

"Yes," she says, then pauses. "Actually, I was wondering if you'd be interested in a position here as student teacher."

"For real, seriously," I say, totally stunned. I really didn't expect to hear this. "So, do you mean like in an actual job working here?"

"Yes, it would be slightly modified, of course, because of your age and experience. But I think we can work something out. So, what do you think?"

I start laughing. "I think that would be awesome."

She nods. "Okay, good. I'll call your grandmother next week and see what we can arrange for after school and weekends. And yes, you will be paid."

"Um, my grandmother will be away all next week. She's leaving tomorrow afternoon."

"Okay, have her call me tomorrow morning. Now it's

not going to be easy. You'll have to pitch in and help out like the rest of us. You'll need to…"

I totally tune out right about now, but I keep nodding and smiling and Ms. Jay keeps talking. I swear I have no idea what she's saying 'cause all I can think about is dancing and getting paid. I'm flying on cloud nine. Who needs coke or meth or pills or any of those other stupid drugs— dancing and getting paid is the biggest high there is. And it's a part-time job doing what I love. I feel like dancing all the way home.

"…so have your grandmother give me a call tomorrow. Okay, then, I'll see you later," Ms. Jay says.

"Okay, I'll make sure she calls you."

She smiles, then turns to go back to her desk. I leave, then open the front door and I see that it's almost dark outside. I know it's not that late so I look at my cell phone, anyway. It's only seven-thirty. Still I'm smiling and energized. I can't wait to tell my grandmother, my sister and my girls. They're all gonna be so thrilled. It looks like my life is finally turning around. Things are going my way. What could seriously go wrong now?

Four

Got Drama?

kenishi_wa K Lewis
*Drama be on my butt chasing me down I like I owe it
money. Every time I think I'm safe and my life is getting back to normal, here it comes again.*
26 Apr * Like * Comment * Share

Shit. Why did I ask that question?

About a block away from my grandmother's house I see
Darien outside again. This time he's leaning against his car
that's parked across the street from his house. Shit. Unfortunately, I have to walk right by his car to get home. That
means walking right by him. Right now I see him before
he sees me. He's talking on his cell phone and he doesn't
look happy. He nods his head and agrees to whatever the
other person is saying.

All of the sudden he starts yelling about money and something not being his fault. I can't tell what else he's talking
about, but I can tell he's pissed. He pushes away from the
side of the car and turns around. He stops yelling and looks
right at me. I'm already looking in his direction, so we eye
each other. His eyes are mean and angry. I have a feeling it's
more to do with seeing me than with the phone call now.

Of course, neither one of us says anything. Our history is way too screwed up and we both know it, so we just stare.

I keep walking, praying he doesn't step up to me. The last thing I want to deal with is Darien in my face, especially when there are no trophies around to grab. The only thing I have is my dance bag and that's useless, so I keep walking. Seconds pass and seem like hours. That's how long it takes for me to walk past him with him watching me the whole time. Thank God my prayer is answered 'cause he doesn't say anything to me.

Then all of the sudden he shifts his weight like he's about to make a move. My heart starts to pound harder, but I can't run. I know he's faster than me. My lungs feel tight as I try to breathe normally, but I can't. Air is getting in but I can't exhale out. I notice there's nobody else around except him and me. He takes two steps away from his car. Shit.

Just then a car horn beeps. I look around quickly. It's Troy, his sister and another little girl. The window is rolled down and he's smiling at me. "Hey, you want a ride home?"

I take a deep, calming breath and try to pull off a smile. I know it comes off halfheartedly, but I don't think Troy notices. He isn't my favorite person, but right now he'll do. "Hey," I say while I keep walking. I glance over at Darien to see what he's doing. He's at the back of his car and he's still staring.

"Do you want a ride?" Troy asks again while driving really slowly beside me. It's obvious he doesn't have a clue what's really going on.

"To whose home?" I ask suspiciously, knowing I have no intention of getting in anybody's car and going anywhere.

Troy smiles and chuckles—he knows exactly what I'm talking about. He's been bugging me since I got to the Penn about going over to his house and hanging out with him. Everybody knows the *real* meaning of "hanging out" with him and I have no intention of being one of his mindless groupies. "Nah, it's not like that, for real. I promise."

"No, thanks," I say while walking and getting farther and farther away from Darien.

"Are you sure?" Troy persists, still driving along slowly beside me.

"Yeah, I'm sure. Thanks, anyway."

"Okay, talk to you later."

He starts driving away and I keep walking. After a while I hear Darien yelling on the phone again. A part of me wants to turn around, but I know I can't. It's like if I do I'll invite him back into my life again and acknowledge that I see him and I seriously don't want that. I just want him to go—to his father's house, to prison, to hell... I really don't care which one.

Now I walk a little faster. But it still feels like Darien is right on my back. I know it's just my imagination, but all I can think about is the night I had to beat him down and everything that happened after that. I know I can't keep being scared. I was never like this before.

Enough, I'm not wasting my time thinking about his stupid ass anymore. I start purposely thinking about my new job at the studio. The closer I get to my grandmother's house the more excited I get to tell her the news. This could change everything. I'll be hanging out at the dance studio plus getting paid. By the time I get to the front door I'm smiling again. I run up the front steps and hurry to the porch. I unlock the door and burst inside, then reset the alarm. "Hello, I'm back," I call out as soon as I walk in and close and lock the front door behind me. There's no answer so I call out again. "Grandmom, I'm home."

I don't smell anything cooking but head straight to the kitchen anyway 'cause that's where she probably is. As soon as I walk in I see she's not there. But there's a note on the table and a plastic-wrapped dish of homemade chocolate chip cookies. There's one thing my grandmother can do and that's cook. For real, the woman is amazing. People stop by the house all the time when she's cooking and baking. They just kick their shoes off under the table, loosen their pants and get busy eating everything in sight.

I keep telling her that she should sell her food and not just give it away for free, but she says God gave her the ability and talent and she can't sell a gift. Yeah, well, I'd be selling food and making some serious bank. I open the refrigerator and check out what we have to eat. It looks like she went shopping and picked up some cold cuts. I fix myself a sandwich and grab some orange juice.

Before I leave the kitchen I check the new double-bolt lock we had put on a few weeks ago. It's solid. The door doesn't budge. Still, I push the trash can in front of the door. It's a habit now. It makes me feel a little safer. I still think if I hadn't done it when they broke into the house before I might never have heard them coming upstairs until it was too late.

I grab my food, then go upstairs. I stop on the second floor and peek into my grandmother's bedroom. The television's on, but she's asleep in her favorite easy chair. She still has her reading glasses on and her Bible on her lap. I walk over and look down at her. She looks so sweet and peaceful, I hate to wake her, but I do anyway. I know she'd want me to. "Grandmom," I say softly, and then repeat it while gently shaking her arm. "Grandmom, I'm home." She opens her eyes and jumps. "Grandmom, it's me, Kenisha," I say. "I'm home."

"Oh, Kenisha," she says sleepily, then sighs. "I guess I must have fallen asleep with my story on." She glances at the television and then at the DVD player clock underneath. "Is that the time?"

"I know I'm late. But it was because I was working—I got a job today."

"A job—where?" she asks suspiciously.

Of course I know why and I guess I don't really blame her for being concerned. The last time I told her I just got a job it was at the pizza place and it got robbed a few days later on my shift. "It's at Freeman Dance Studio," I say quickly, then sit down on the bed beside her chair. "A couple of the dance instructors couldn't make it, so Ms. Jay asked me if I would take one of the hip-hop classes. I did and I was really good. Everybody said so. When the class was over she asked me if I'd be interested in teaching hip-hop part-time. She'd like you to call her tomorrow."

She smiles, seeing how excited I am. "It sounds perfect for you, but what about school?"

"No, this would only be in the evenings and on weekends. And I'll make sure it doesn't interfere with school and doing homework. So can I do it? I promise my grades won't drop."

"Let me think about it overnight. I'll speak with Ms. Jay tomorrow," she says.

I nod slowly. All my excitement is gone. "Okay."

"Kenisha, I'm not saying no. I just need to know more about what's expected of you. Part-time jobs have a way of becoming full-time jobs especially when you're young. I don't want you taken advantage of."

I nod. I guess that sounds a little better. "I know," I say, then look around her room. Two suitcases are on the floor. One's open and empty. "Are you getting everything together for your trip next week?"

"Yes, Lord. I still have a few more things to do."

"When are you packing?"

"I'll pack tomorrow afternoon."

"Do you need any help?"

"No, I'll be fine. Are you going to be okay here by yourself tomorrow night? Jade said she'd come early if you need her."

"Grandmom, I'll be fine. I'm sixteen years old. I've stayed in the house by myself before. It's no big deal." She looks at me and I can see the wondering in her eyes. She's not sure. "You should go and enjoy your trip. I'll be fine. I promise." She nods hesitantly. I can see she's not completely assured. "Okay, I'm going up to my room. I have a reading assignment to do," I say, standing and walking over to the bedroom door.

"Did you get something to eat?" she asks me.

"I made a sandwich. Do you want me to make you one?"

"No, I'm fine. I ate earlier." She covers her mouth and yawns. "Oh, my, I guess I didn't realize I was as tired as I am. I think I'm gonna turn in early. I have a big day tomorrow. Don't you stay up too late—you have school tomorrow. Good night."

"I know. I won't. Good night, Grandmom," I say, and go up to my room. I drop my backpack and dance bag on the floor by the bed, then put my sandwich and juice on the desk. I sit down, take a bite of my sandwich, then plug my cell phone into the charger and open my laptop.

I go online. My first stop is always Facebook. I confirm three friend requests, then check out my messages. I swear I have no idea how people lived without social networking. What did they do—just sit in a dark room and stare at the walls? So anyway, I check out my home page to see what's happening and who's talking. Boring. There's nobody interesting on. I exit and hit up Twitter. Boring.

Bummer. Both sites are slow with nobody saying anything interesting. I read a few posts from people I know but decide not to respond. I usually only tweet with my girls, Jalisa and Diamond, and neither one is on the network right now. I check out the hip-hop sites I usually visit. Then a few minutes later my cell phone rings. It's Jalisa and Diamond. "Oh, my God, I was just gonna call. You'll never guess what happened today—I got a job."

"For real," Diamond says excitedly.

"Cool, where?" Jalisa asks. "But wait, I hope it's not back at the pizza place like before 'cause that was too insane."

"No, it's at Freeman Dance Studio. I'm gonna teach dance."

"No way," Diamond says.

Jalisa just starts laughing out loud. "No, she's not. She's just messing with us."

"No, for real, Ms. Jay asked me today. I went there after school and a couple of teachers couldn't make it in, so she asked me to help out and teach one of the beginning hip-hop classes. I did it and she asked me if I wanted to teach at the school part-time. I said yes."

"What about us?" Jalisa asks.

"What do you mean?" I ask.

"*Unus pro omnibus, omnes pro uno*—does that ring a bell to you?" Diamond says.

"I know, right," Jalisa adds, "so just you."

"Yeah, just me. Why not just me? What, you saying I'm not good enough?" The line went silent on both sides. All of a sudden I got it. They don't think I'm a good enough dancer to teach. "I can't believe y'all are hatin' on me like this. I thought you were my girls and you'd be happy for me. I guess not." Okay, now this is starting to feel weird.

"It's not about hatin'…" Diamond starts saying.

Right now I'm not in the mood to be hearing either one of them. "No, I got it. I understand. You don't think I'm good enough to teach a class, right."

"Ain't nobody saying that, Kenisha," Jalisa says.

"Then what?" I ask, knowing there's nothing either one of them can say at this point to fix this. The line was quiet again. "Whatever. I gotta go." I hang up. Shit. My cell rings again. It's Diamond. I let it go to voice mail. I don't feel like being bothered. I plug my phone back in the charger, then open my book to read my assignment. I finish my sandwich and drink my juice while I read and answer the questions. I figure I can check them over in first period 'cause I'm really tired now. I put my stuff away and lie across my bed, checking out Twitter and Facebook one last time. Both Diamond and Jalisa left messages that I don't answer.

I type out and send my sister, Jade, a Facebook private message about my new job, then just as I'm describing the class I taught today I get a chat alert. I don't pay attention at first 'cause I figure it's either Diamond or Jalisa. After a few minutes it beeps again. I pull up the little box in the corner and I stop cold when I see the name.

Hey. It's a simple message, but it shocks me seeing who

sent it. For a few seconds I just sit there staring at the single word. It's from Troy Carson. I know you're there.

I'm here, I type slowly, then press the enter key.

What are you doing?

I'm typing a message.

To who? Him? he types.

Of course I know exactly who he is talking about—Terrence. But I'm not gonna let him know I was typing a message to my sister. Why do you want to know?

I'm curious.

Well, then, it's none of your business.

Tell me, I want to know.

Get used to disappointment.

Are you telling him about us?

I laugh out loud. I see you have jokes now. Us—there is no us. We attend the same school, that's all.

Are you sure?

I wait a few seconds, then respond with my own question. So what's with all the being nice to me now? We were never exactly best buds before. We despise each other, remember.

I wait a few seconds, then a few seconds more. After a

while I realize he's not gonna respond to my comment. I look at the words I just typed. It's the truth. Troy and I have always been at opposite points. Our lockers are the only thing that connects us. He's a popular football star with a lot more smarts than he lets people see and he's got just about every girl in the building falling at his feet—except me.

Everybody knows him. He's the school's quarterback and track star. He's also the only seventeen-year-old junior who already has a five-year scholarship to an Ivy League university on lockdown. He's tall and handsome and both his stepmother and father make big bank. He's popular and everybody likes him. He can have any girl in school, so why is he all up on me? I don't know the answer to that question and I'm not sure he does, either. And bottom line, I'm still not sure this isn't one of his stupid childish games.

Not despise, he eventually types.

Then what? Why?

Truthfully, I don't know. I guess it's 'cause you get me.

So what, I figured out that he pretends to be a dumb jock, but in reality he's a lot smarter than anyone thinks. Wrong, I don't get you. I just know the game you play.

Yes, you do. Yeah, I know I can be slightly insensitive and I have an ego, but…

Slightly insensitive, I repeat, just slightly, is that all? LOL. Okay, maybe a little more than slightly, he types. Either way you get me and that's why you're scared of me.

You obvious think you're talking to someone else 'cause I am NOT scared of you.

Yes, you are. You're scared of getting close to me.

Why would I want to do that?

Because we both know that there's more to us than what other people see. I know it and you know it.

Yeah, but I know you, Troy. And given our past and your reputation, I'd say you probably have about ten football players standing around your computer right now laughing about all this. Having fun, boys?

Now you're blocking. You know you're wrong and that scares you, too. What if I don't and I'm here in my bedroom all by myself thinking about you? What if this is who I am? What if the Troy you think you know isn't really me? What if I'm exactly what you don't want me to be because you're scared it's true?

Shit. Now he's officially starting to scare me 'cause he's right. I don't want him to be different. I need him to be an asshole like always. The thing is, I don't want to think about him at all. At least, not like that.

You like me. You know it. Just admit it, he types.

Shit. My stomach jumps like I just dropped from a fifty-foot roller coaster on free fall. I stare at the box and read his words once more. I type something and then delete it. I go to type something else, then stop because I have no idea what I'm doing. Just then another chat box opens up with one word. Hey.

It's Terrence. I type, answering him immediately. Hey!

I just got back to the dorm room.

Working? I ask.
Studying, he types.

Tired?

Yep.

What's up for this weekend? Are you coming home? I ask.
There's a party off campus on Saturday at my frat brother's house. I think it's close to your house in VA, he posts.
I pause for a moment. So much for hoping he'd say yes. You going? I type hesitantly.

Yep, definitely. I'm not working Saturday. It's supposed to be really nice. Taj is performing on campus and I heard she's supposed to stop by the party afterward. My frat brothers are putting it together, so I kinda gotta be there.

Taj!

Yeah, she used to go to the Penn back in the day. She dropped out right after she did her first music video.

I didn't know that. So do you know her?

Yeah, kinda, we were in different circles. She's younger than me, but she was always around the way hanging out.

That's right. I forgot, she's my age.

Seeing her...hard to believe.

I know, right. She looks way older in her makeup, wigs and costumes. So, do you like her music?

It's all right. I liked her first CD, the one Tyrece produced. Now she's just commercial.

So, what's she like?

Back then she was out of control. All she ever talked about was being a star.

So you know her kinda well.

She had a crush on most of the guys around the way.

A crush, huh, even on you?

Yeah, we kicked it for a minute.

I don't type anything else. Everyone knows Taj is a wild thing. Her reputation is fierce in the media. My sister's boyfriend, Ty, discovered her and produced her first CD. As soon as her first song hit platinum she dropped him and went with a bigger producer and record label. She constantly changes her persona and gets more and more outlandish. I know Terrence wants to see her, most guys do. I also notice he doesn't ask me to go with him to the party. Suddenly it's obvious he doesn't want me there. Sounds like fun, I finally type.

Yeah, it should be. You want to come with? he posts.

I start smiling. I want to scream, *Hell, yeah!* But I stay calm. Yeah, I'm coming with.

Good.

A chat box from both Jalisa and Diamond pop up. I ignore them and keep chatting with Terrence. I'm still kinda pissed at them. Hey, I forgot to tell you, I got a job, I post.

Where?

Freeman Dance. I'm gonna teach beginning hip-hop.

Yeah, I can see that. You're a great dancer.

The smile on my face gets wider. It's nice to know somebody thinks I can dance. We keep chatting about my new job and about other things. Then he says he has to study for an exam tomorrow. I'll call you tomorrow.

Okay. See ya. Miss you.

Miss you 2.

Smiling, I close his box and see Troy's chat box is still there. I forgot all about him. I see his last post. You still there? he typed. I guess it was a while ago, so I decide not to answer. I don't know what game he's playing so I just ignore him as usual and go back to Twitter. Jalisa and Diamond are on.

Seriously, I have no idea what their drama is. I thought they'd be happy for me to be teaching at Freeman, but obviously not. I guess they noticed I was on 'cause they tweet one word—Call.

I think about it a few minutes and decide to call. We've been friends too long for me not to. I go to grab my cell just as it rings. I check caller ID. It's Diamond, so I answer. Jalisa is there, too. I start right in. "I can't believe y'all are hating on me like this. I would never do that to you." Neither one says anything. "So y'all really don't think I'm good enough."

"It's not about being good enough," Diamond says.

"You know you're good, so stop frontin'," Jalisa adds.

"So what's your problem, then?" I ask.

"We promised one another," Diamond says. "*Unus pro omnibus, omnes pro uno*—one for all, all for one.'"

"What?" I ask.

"We always said that we were going to do everything together, especially when it comes to dance. Now you're doing this by yourself and dissing us," Jalisa says.

All of the sudden I get it. We did promise. "Okay, I know. But Ms. Jay asked me because I was there and she needed somebody. If y'all was there she would have asked you, too. Plus, she knows that I need a job after everything that happened at the pizza place." They don't say anything after that, so I just start talking. "Anyway, I don't know how long its gonna last."

"Why won't it last?" Diamond asks.

"The roof is leaking and the third floor flooded again. The floors are all messed up."

"Our studio, too?" Jalisa asks.

"Yeah, there, too."

"When's she gonna get it fixed?"

"That's just it, she may not. She said she's thinking about closing the dance studio down," I say.

"That's great. Seriously, she could do so much better someplace else. She could even find a building here in Virginia. That one is always falling apart and something's always messed up there," Diamond says.

"I know, right," Jalisa adds. "In the winter it's freezing and in the summer it's burning up. And the roof is forever leaking, so the dance floors are always slightly buckled. How are we supposed to practice and dance on floors like that?"

"No, she didn't say she was moving, she said she was thinking about closing it down, like permanently—like no more Freeman Dance Studio at all."

"What?" they both say.

"Yeah, I know, that's what I said. I asked her about putting on some kind of talent show with judges and everything to raise money. She said maybe it was a good idea. So maybe she's gonna do it. I told her we'd help if she does."

"Yeah, we can help."

Right then we started making all kinds of plans. A half hour later we had it all hooked up including the promotions, decorations and who we wanted on the planning committee with us. I was gonna ask Jade about getting Tyrece and Gayle to be judges and maybe ask some of their friends, too. We decided we'd open the show with the dance we've been practicing and also decided to go to Freeman tomorrow to practice more. It was late when we finally got finished talking. After a while we hung up and, not surprisingly, started texting.

FIVE

Wake-up Call

kenishi_wa K Lewis
There's nothing like waking up to an exciting new day—new challenges and new adventures. For the record, this is nothing like it.
27 Apr * Like * Comment * Share

I hate everything about Fridays that involves going to school and dealing with drama. Add to that, this morning I'm already exhausted. I stayed up way too late last night talking with Terrence and then with Jalisa and Diamond. So now I can't keep my eyes open. My physics teacher, Mr. Maynard, is standing in front of the class. I have no idea what he's talking about and I'm totally distracted. I just can't seem to focus. Not because second period is long and mind-numbingly boring and not because it's raining and it's Friday and I'd rather be just about anyplace else than here, but because of my mom.

I dreamed about her again last night and then after that I couldn't go back to sleep. I just stayed up and stared out my bedroom window the rest of the night. It wasn't exactly like the other dreams I've been having about her, but it had the same idea. We were together and then we weren't.

In this dream we were sitting on the D.C. Metro train together going someplace. We were all dressed up, looking good and having fun. We were talking and I was telling her everything that had been going on with me. She didn't really speak, but I knew what she was saying. She told me she was fine now and that everything was going to be okay with me, but that I have to do something else. But I couldn't hear what she was saying 'cause the train was really loud as it was coming to the station.

I told her about my dad and his girlfriend, Courtney, and how I slapped her face. Her eyes lit up. I knew she loved it. Then I told her about how I hit Darien and broke his arm with one of his trophies. I didn't tell her everything else that happened, but I have a feeling she already knew. I told her Jade was doing well and that having her as my sister was the best thing to happen to me. I saw tears in her eyes and wanted to ask her why she was so sad, but I ran out of time.

The train stopped and the doors opened. I got up to get off, but she stayed on. I turned around and started back to be with her just as the doors were closing. I called out to her. She smiled and shook her head. She waved and told me that I couldn't go with her and that she couldn't stay with me. I knew what she meant 'cause I know she's dead, but it still makes me really sad to know that I had to say goodbye to her all over again. Then the doors closed and I stood there on the platform and watched the train disappear into the dark tunnel, not knowing if I'd ever see her again, even in my dreams. I hope so.

After that I woke up. I didn't know it, but I was crying in my sleep. It wasn't really a feeling bad kinda crying. Yes, I miss her; yes, I want her to still be in my life; but I was crying because I was happy. I like how I get to see and talk to her in my dreams. For that short time it's private. She's all mine. I know seeing her and being with her isn't real, but for just those few moments, it the realest thing in the world to me.

So now I'm stuck in class with my chin in the palm of my hand, listening to my teacher talk about something nobody really cares about. My cell phone vibrates just as I'm about to doze off. I look around to see who saw my head jerk up, but I notice just about everybody around me half-asleep, too. I pull out my cell and check out the text message. It's from Li'l T. Seriously. I don't know how he got my cell number. Anyway, I read his text. I did it. Did you see? You're up!

Okay, as usual I don't have a clue what he's talking about. I figure it's another one of his mini dramas or something and just ignore it. Just then another text comes in from him. It's an attachment, but I just ignore it, as well. I'm too tired to play his games.

A few seconds later the classroom door opens and everyone lazily turns or looks up. This girl walks in and looks around nervously. She walks over and hands Mr. Maynard her schedule. He glances at it, then hands it back to her and tells her to have a seat. She walks over near me and sits down, looking straight ahead.

Everybody starts staring and whispering. After a while the room gets louder and louder. Mr. Maynard turns around and claps his hands. "All right, all right, settle down. Yes, we have a new student. Yes, we can all get acquainted after class. Right now, let's get back to Newton's three laws of motion." He turns his attention back to the board and everybody starts talking again.

I start smiling and look over. I know her. It's Neeka Reynolds. She used to go to Hazelhurst with me. She's a friend, but not a close inner circle kinda friend. It's not because we had problems or anything like that, we didn't. We just never got tight like that. I have my girls, Jalisa and Diamond, and she has hers. She used to be friends with Chili and Regan, but now she's not, I think. I can't stand both girls.

Neeka looks around the room and finally sees me. Her jaw drops and we start smiling at each other. I mouth, "Hi."

She waves and mouths, "Hey, what are you doing here?"

I start laughing and give her the "duh" look. She laughs, too. Mr. Maynard walks over and places a beat-up-looking textbook on her desk while he's talking about Newton's second law of motion. She makes a face at the messed-up book. I start laughing again. I know exactly what she means. At Hazelhurst we always had brand-new textbooks—a set to use in class and then one to take and leave at home for homework assignments.

"We gotta talk," she mouths.

I nod my head. "Definitely, when did you get here?"

"Tuesday, my schedule is still all messed up right now."

"Did you move to D.C.?" I ask. She nods. "Close to here?" She nods again and glances up at Mr. Maynard as he turns to face the class again. I turn around, too. Some of the other kids in the class are also paying attention now. Maynard is talking about an exam next week and passing out a study sheet that will require us to fill in the answers. We start paying attention, then the bell rings. Everyone quickly gets up and starts walking to the door. Mr. Maynard keeps talking about the exam next week and to make sure we fill out our study sheets.

Neeka and I get up and meet midway in the aisle. We laugh and hug each other. I don't know which one of us is more excited to see the other. "I can't believe you're here," I say, smiling.

"I know, right," Neeka says, still laughing.

"Come on, we gotta go. The late bell rings in seven minutes, but it feels like two because of all these little freshman who don't know how to walk." We laugh and then start heading to the door. "What's your next class?" I ask.

Neeka pulls out her schedule and looks at it. I peek over her shoulder. "Third period, U.S. History with Ms. Grayson," she says, looking up and down the now-crowded hall. "Do you know her?"

I smile and nod. "Yeah, she's okay. I have her for U.S. History, too, but opposite days than you. Come on, I'll walk you to her class. I have to go that way." We start walking and some of the football players I always see hanging with Troy start staring and smiling at us as they pass. I figure it has something to do with the conversation Troy and I had last night. I knew I was right. He is an ass. I just shake my head. "Ignore the staring. Welcome to the Penitentiary."

"The Penitentiary. Somebody else called it that. Why?"

"They say this building was supposed to be a penitentiary way back when they started building it, but then they turned it into a high school instead. That's why it's built so much like a prison. But it's really because it's named for William Penn Hall. What do you think of it so far?"

"It's okay, definitely not Hazelhurst." She smiles, still looking around. "I guess it could be worse and of course there are—" she says as she eyes this guy walking toward us and he eyes us. She turns when he passes and he turns, too "—some seriously fine-ass brothas going here."

I forgot Neeka has one of those reputations. She's not exactly a total slut like Chili, but she's definitely on her way. Both her parents are mixed black and white. She could seriously pass for white if she wanted to. She's got blue eyes, short wavy black hair and light skin. She also has a big butt and big chest and doesn't mind showing either.

I shake my head as I watch her staring at the guys walking down the hall. She is definitely not ready for this. All that stuff she used to do at Hazelhurst will for sure get her ass kicked here. "You need to chill on that," I warn her.

"What?" she asks innocently.

"You know what. Some of these silly-ass girls don't play, especially when it comes to these guys. They do a serious lockdown hold and if they think you're trying to step in on their guy, they will definitely come after you loaded. And that's not just a figure of speech. There are girl-on-girl fights almost every day because of some guy steppin' out. Trust me, it's not worth it," I say. She shrugs. I know right then she wasn't hearing me, so I just drop it. I warned her, that's all I can do. Just then my cell phone vibrates in my pocket again. I check while still walking Neeka to class. It was Li'l T again. He sent another email with an attachment. I'll check it out later.

"So, when's your lunch period?" I ask Neeka.

She checks her schedule again. "After this, fourth period."

"Me, too. I'll meet you in the upstairs cafeteria. We gotta talk. There's Grayson's class right there," I say, then stop walking and point. I didn't go any closer 'cause I didn't want to see her. "I gotta go this way. My next class is downstairs. I'll see you at lunch."

"All right, see you," she says, then turns to Ms. Grayson's classroom. I head to the stairs, then turn when I hear

Neeka call my name. "Kenisha, hey, I forgot to tell you. I saw you on YouTube last night. Damn, girl, you are really good. I didn't even think it was you at first."

"Me what?" I ask.

"Hello, Kenisha."

I turn, seeing Ms. Grayson come out of her classroom to stand in the hall like she usually does. Most teachers do it to make sure there's no trouble in the halls. It doesn't work.

"Hi, Ms. Grayson," I say, then turn back to Neeka, waiting for her to tell me what she's talking about—me on You-Tube.

"I understand you missed my class yesterday," Ms. Grayson adds, looking right at me.

I roll my eyes. *Not now,* I think to myself as I consider just walking away. But I know Ms. Grayson. She doesn't give up on anything that easily. So just ignoring her, hoping she'll go away, isn't going to do it. I turn to her. "I know. I forgot to get a note. I had an appointment with my doctor yesterday afternoon." It was the truth. I did have an appointment with Tubbs. I figure she doesn't have to know that I didn't go.

"Okay, make sure you get me a note for the absence so I don't keep you marked as unexcused absent."

"I will," I say just as Neeka gives her the schedule. Ms. Grayson checks out the schedule, then gives it back.

"I'll see you at lunch," Neeka says, then goes inside.

"Kenisha, get to class," Ms. Grayson says.

Damn. I still have no idea what Neeka's talking about—me on YouTube last night. What does that mean? I didn't put anything up on YouTube. My cell phone vibrates again. I can't answer because I know I need to make it to class or be late. I hurry downstairs and get to my classroom.

A lot of students are already seated. I sit down and then check my cell. I have a text message from Jade, Jalisa and Diamond and a tweet from Li'l T. I check out Jade's, Diamond's and Jalisa's messages. They all ask me about YouTube. Okay, now this is getting too weird. I have no idea what's happening on YouTube! I check out Li'l T's first message and open his attachment. My jaw drops. Oh, shit! Just wait until I get my hands on him. I swear, I'm gonna strangle him.

The late bell rings. I look up—everybody's in class and our teacher clears his throat. "All right, class, settle down. Let's get started. Open your textbooks to page…"

kenishi_wa K Lewis
@Lil_T_istheman *i told you not to video me and you did it, anyway. plus you put it up on youtube! you are in so much trouble!* 55 minutes ago

SIX

Screamin' Out Loud

kenishi_wa K Lewis
Finding your voice isn't all that hard to do. You just have to look deep down inside and free your pain. After that, just let it loose. If you're lucky, somebody will hear you.
27 Apr * Like * Comment * Share

kenishi_wa K Lewis
@Lil_T_istheman *where are you?!* 1 minute ago

All through class I keep thinking about what I saw—me dancing on stage. Near the end of class I leave another text message for Li'l T. Then as soon as the fourth period bell rings I start looking for him. I check all of his usual hangouts—the weight room, the school nurse, the library and, of course, the area right outside the girls' locker room. I can't find him anywhere. He knows I'm pissed. That's why his chicken ass is hiding from me.

Six text messages and two phone calls later, I'm still waiting for him to hit me up. Any other time he'd be all over me, up in my business and getting on my nerves. But now he's nowhere in sight. Next I head to the first-floor cafeteria.

It's the first lunch of the day and I've seen him hanging out down here a few times. I'm not sure what his schedule is or what classes he has, but I know he sometimes stops by to hang with his friends. But of course today he's not here.

I walk past the lunch line and look around. Then I see two of his friends sitting at a lunch table, talking and eating their food, so I go over to them. "Hey, have y'all seen Li'l T?" I ask. They look at each other and then up at me like I'm speaking a foreign language. "Hello," I say slower, "have you seen Li'l T?"

They look at each other again and I know there's a lie coming. "Uh, nah, we ain't seen him all day. I don't know if he came to school today."

"Yeah, I think he's home sick today," the other one adds, and then glances at his friend and starts eating again.

I know they're lying. "Well, when you see him, tell him Kenisha is looking for him." Neither acknowledges my request one way or the other, so I scan the room one more time. Then I see Neeka walk into the cafeteria and look around. I forgot all about meeting her. I head over to her.

"Hey, there you are," she says, coming in the door just as I was leaving. "I thought you said you'd be at the second-floor cafeteria."

"I did. I came down looking for this guy, but he's not here," I say, looking around one last time before heading out. "Come on. The lines upstairs are always shorter by now." We go upstairs and get in the lunch line. Pizza, chicken tenders, subs and Stromboli are the top choices. We each get a slice of pizza and grab a bottle of water, then find a seat in the back of the cafeteria.

"Are you okay? You look pissed," Neeka asks.

"I'm fine, just more stupid drama to deal with."

She shakes her head. "Yeah, I know how that goes. I'm so sick of dealing with other people's drama interrupting my life."

"I know, right," I say.

"That's why I'm so glad to be out of Hazelhurst."

"Why, what happened?" I ask.

"Just stupid stuff," she says without saying much more. "I got into a fight and you know their 'zero tolerance' rule...."

"Yeah, I know that rule too well." We laugh 'cause just about everybody knows why I got kicked out of Hazelhurst.

"Girl, I saw that fight you had with Regan at the beginning of the school year. I used to hang with her, but I can't deal with her stuck-up, wannabe drama now. She'd never admit it but everyone knows you kicked her ass. They're still talking about that. They call her 'hallway hair' and you know they still be picking weave up off the floor, don't you?"

We really laugh this time. Then I just shake my head, thinking while she keeps talking. The thing is the fight was stupid and a bad decision on my part. It wasn't really my fault—well, maybe some of it was. Regan said something about my mother and it was way too soon to be messing with me about that. It pissed me off, so I hit her. I just didn't stop.

My grandmother was right. Life's all about the decisions we make and the consequences that follow. That one instantly changed my life and like a pebble in a pond it's still rippling wider and wider. But it's over with now. And at least I don't have to deal with Regan ever again. "So did your family move here or are you still living in Virginia?" I ask her.

"My dad's military. He's doing another tour overseas.

My mom and I just moved to D.C. to be closer to her job. It was either stay at Hazelhurst and commute, or go to private school here in D.C."

"This isn't private. Why not go to another private here?"

"To tell you the truth, I'm tired of private schools. That's all I've ever gone to—all girls and private. Boring," she says. "I want something different."

"So you came here," I say, shaking my head, not getting it. "I don't know why anyone would choose to come here of all places. It's like the worst school in the city."

"What do you mean? Penn Hall is one of the top rated and one of the best public schools in the district."

"Top rated, one of the best, no way. Who told you that?" I ask, trying my best not to burst out laughing in her face 'cause she seriously got played with some messed-up information.

"My mom and I checked it out. Penn Hall is a public school for neighborhood kids, but it's also a magnet school for exceptional students. Students from all over the city get vouchers to come here, so it's right up there with the best."

Okay, all that sounds too weird. I never heard anything like that before. This is just a regular old inner-city high school—no big deal. I'm thinking Neeka has her facts all screwed up. This is definitely not the school she thinks it is. There's nothing exceptional about this place or its students.

"Hey. What's up?"

I turn, seeing Ursula sit down across from me. She's sipping on a fruit juice while texting. "Hey," I say, and then try texting Li'l T yet again.

"I'm Ursula," she says to Neeka.

"Yeah, I think you're in my chemistry class next period," Neeka says.

"I think so, too." Ursula sips her drink again.

"Ursula, this is Neeka. She and I used to go to the same school in Virginia."

"When'd you transfer in?"

"Tuesday, but they keep messing with my schedule. I've had three class schedules already. Half the time I have no idea where I'm supposed to be."

"Hazelhurst, right?" We both nod. "Damn, what are they doing over there?" Ursula says to us. We look at her confused. She shakes her head, smiling. "It must be an epidemic or something. There was a girl in my last class who just transferred here from there, too."

"From Hazelhurst— Who?" I ask. She shrugs, shaking her head.

I look at Neeka. She chuckles to herself, then smiles. "Wouldn't it be funny if it was Regan and then you'd..." Neeka stops talking and holds her hand to her mouth. "Oh, shit, that's right. I almost forgot about that. I heard she was leaving Hazelhurst, but I have no idea where she's going. Oh, shit."

I just look at her, shaking my head. "No, Neeka, it wouldn't be funny," I say. Having Regan Payne come to the Penn would be almost as bad as having Chili Rodriguez come here. I hate both of them.

"Who's Regan?" Ursula asks, putting her cell phone down.

"Nobody," I say quickly. Neeka starts laughing.

"What?" Ursula says, looking at us. "Tell me, what?"

I roll my eyes. "Fine, whatever," I say.

Neeka leans in close and so does Ursula. I drink the rest

of my drink and try to ignore them. "Okay," Neeka begins, "at the beginning of the school year Kenisha and Regan got into a fight. It was huge. The whole school knew about it. Kenisha got kicked out of school but Regan didn't, even though everyone knows she started it. But her uncle or cousin or something like that is on the board of directors.

"Anyway, Regan used to have all this long hair and she always said it was hers. So while they were fighting Kenisha grabbed her hoodie and then yanked her weave out. There was fake hair all over the hallway. They still joke about Regan's weave being on the floor. They call her 'hallway hair.' Like if you're late for class they say, 'I tripped on Regan's hair.'" Neeka was laughing so hard she barely got the story out and Ursula was almost in tears. Students around us started turning around staring.

Okay, yeah, I was laughing, too, but seriously, I wasn't feeling the other part. Regan. Here. Hell, no. Then all of the sudden I remember why me and Neeka never became good friends. She's a'ight and all, but she just can't keep her big mouth shut.

So we're still talking about hanging out at Hazelhurst and the students there when I see Troy come in the cafeteria. He looks around and then he sees me. He starts walking toward our table. I immediately start praying he keeps on walking, but I have a feeling he won't. As usual, most of the girls sitting at the tables around mine stop what they're doing and just start whispering and staring at him. I shake my head. No wonder he has the ego he has.

So he comes over and sits down right next to me. He doesn't say anything. He just eyes me and smiles. Just about everybody around us stares and starts whispering. It's obvious they're talking about me. Even Neeka and Ursula are smiling like they all of the sudden know something. Troy just keeps staring at me. "Yes?" I say, finally turning to him.

He smiles. His deep dimples pierce his cheeks. "Are you finally answering my question from last night?"

"What question?" I ask. He just smiles, stands up and walks away. "Whatever." I shake my head. I'm pissed, 'cause he knows exactly what he just did. He started everybody talking about us and I know that's exactly what he wants.

"Oh, my God, who the hell is that? Is he the guy you were looking for downstairs?" Neeka asks with an expression on her face that I know too well. It's the same look on the face of most of the girls at the school whenever Troy walks by.

"Hell, no," I say.

"That's Troy Dawson," Ursula adds with unneeded emphasis.

"Damn, he is gorgeous. Are y'all hanging out?"

"No, definitely not," I say.

"Girl, you should get with him. He's obviously interested."

"But I'm not and he's definitely not my type."

Ursula laughs. "Excuse me, but Troy is every girl's type."

"Well, not mine. Besides, I already have someone— remember Terrence? He's in college and we're—" Just then the first bell rings. We quickly grab our books, dump our trays and head out. "I'll see you later."

"Okay, see you later," Ursula and Neeka say, heading to their class. As soon as I leave the cafeteria I see Troy down the hall. He looks at me and smiles knowingly. I just shake my head and keep walking. I have no idea what his problem is or what he thinks he's doing and I really don't care.

My cell vibrates. I check it. I have a text message from

Li'l T. I hurry to class. The door is open and the lights are on. I go in and take my seat. Right now I'm the only one here. I pull my cell out, sit down in my seat and read his message. Hey, K, I hear you're looking for me.

I roll my eyes and start typing as fast as I can just as a few more students start coming into the classroom. Where are you? I type.

Had an appointment today, he types. Did you see it?

Yeah.

What do you think?

Take it down now!

seven

Are You Nuts?

Thankfully my last two classes of the day fly by fast. Before I know it the bell rings and I'm the first person out of the room. My locker is right down the hall, so I get there, toss the books I don't need in, grab what I do and then get out of there. As soon as I slam my locker closed and head to the exit my cell vibrates. I get outside and answer. I know its Li'l T, so I don't even check my caller ID. I'm wrong. It's not. "Baby girl."

Crap. As soon as I hear my dad's nickname for me I know I've got drama coming. He's like that. Drama follows him like a twelve-o'clock shadow—it's always right under his feet. Of course he brings it all on himself. His life is nothing but stupid "baby mama" drama on top of "I can only think about myself" drama with an extra large helping of "I just can't step up and be a man" drama.

But that was before. Now he's been ignoring me for weeks. Every since we caught Courtney, his girlfriend, in his office about to do the nasty with her lawyer on his desk, he's been acting all "I'm gonna be a real father." She does whatever he says and he likes it. He tells her to jump and she starts jumping jacks. It's pathetic, so I haven't been there to visit in a while. I do miss my little brothers, though.

But the funny thing is he expects me to just roll over and go along with it—not. I still laugh about that shit.

"Baby girl, are you there?" he says.

"Yeah, hi, Dad, what's up?" I say, already expecting drama. My voice is low and barely audible.

"Can you hear me? I'm gonna pick you up from school today, so I want you to wait for me. I'll meet you right outside. I'm leaving the office now so I should be there in about fifteen minutes."

First of all, what, is he nuts? Does he really expect me to be sitting around outside of this school building waiting for him to pick me up like I'm in kindergarten? See, I knew his drama was gonna try and turn into my drama. I seriously do not want to be waiting outside for my dad to pick me up from school. Then secondly, there's no way he's gonna be here in fifteen minutes. D.C. going home on a Friday after work means traffic in the city is insane—he'd be lucky if he gets here in half an hour. Either way it's not going to happen. "Kenisha. Kenisha. Are you there?" I'm so busy being annoyed that I forget to answer him. "Kenisha?"

I smile. "Dad, if you're still there I can barely hear you." I talk louder. He starts to repeat what he just said and I just smile to myself. I interrupt him midway. "Dad, listen I'm headed home from school now. I'll call you when I get to

Grandmom's house. Okay, see ya." I end the call and keep walking. A block from the house I see Li'l T on the other side of the street. He's talking with a couple of guys I don't recognize. I call out to him. He turns and waves. I get ready to cross the street, but I see him shaking hands and bumping shoulders with the guys and then he turns to come across the street to meet me. I wait for him as traffic passes and he weaves his way through. He's smiling as he approaches. "Hey, did you see it?" he yells as he crosses. I can't believe it—he's all excited.

"Yeah, I saw it. How you gonna put me on blast like that when I specifically told you not to. Are you out of your friggin' mind?" I snap as soon as he's closer.

"Whoa, hold up, girl. You don't need to be coming at me with all that hostility when I'm just trying to do you a favor."

"A favor," I repeat, astonished by his plan.

"Yeah, a favor. This video is gonna open all kinds of doors for us. With you dancing and me producing, we'll be famous. I'm talking pulling down some serious cash money."

He looks at me all innocent and then he starts laughing. I swear I am two seconds from beating him down right here and now. "What is wrong with you? I can't believe you did that to me. I told you no taping, didn't I, and you did it, anyway. You need to take that down now."

"Take it down, no way. Come on, girl, you said I could put it up. You said, 'Yeah, right, you do that.' So I did."

Crap, I remember I did say that. "I was being sarcastic."

"Seriously, you looked great up there or else I wouldn't have taped you and uploaded it in the first place. Do you see all the hits we're getting already? You went from over two hundred views yesterday to almost a hundred thousand views in only two days. You're on track, girl. You're on the front page of YouTube and I swear we're about to go viral."

"I don't care about getting hits and going viral. It's not supposed to be there. Get rid of it."

"Okay, now we need to talk percentage here. I think as your promoter, videographer, producer, editor and manager I need to be pulling down, like, forty percent of the take, right."

"Are you deaf now or something? I just told you to take it down. You can't just video tape someone without their knowledge or permission and put it up on the internet."

"Sure I can. People do it all the time."

"Take it down," I insist.

"See, you wrong. You're just saying that now, but as soon as we go viral and everybody hits it up you'll be thanking me."

"Hell, no, take it down now!"

He looked shocked. "What do you mean?" he asks innocently.

"Did I stutter? What do you mean, what do I mean? It's simple. The same way you put it up there you can take it down."

He looks away and shrugs. "I can't."

"What do you mean you can't? Just do it."

"I don't know how," he confesses.

There's no way I believe him. "Yes, you do," I say.

"No, seriously, I don't. I've put things up before, but I've never had to take anything down."

"Well, just do the opposite of what you did to put it up."

"You know it don't work like that. It's not that easy."

I give him one of those looks, so that he knows I'm serious. "I'm not playing, Jerome Tyler. Take it down."

"Okay, okay, I'll do it. But seriously, the least you can say is thank you."

"Thank you for what?" I ask. "For messing with my life even though I specifically told you not to?"

"Girl, you don't even know, I'm about to make you famous. Do you know how many people made it big by doing a YouTube video and it going viral? Look at Taj. She did it the same way and look how famous she is."

"Do I look like I want to be famous? I didn't ask you to put it up there, so why should I thank you for taking it down? Just do it." I start walking away from him 'cause he's getting on my last nerve right now.

"Yeah, a'ight, fine, whatever..." he calls out as I keep walking away. "But see, I was only trying to do you a favor. I was gonna make you a star. And don't tell me you don't want to be famous. I know you do, everybody does...."

He keeps talking his talk and I keep walking away. I'm so not listening to him anymore. I said what I had to say and now I'm done. I don't care if he's pissed. I'm pissed, too.

So as soon as I turn the corner I see my dad's car parked in front of my grandmother's house. Shit. I figured I'd have enough time to get in and out before he got here, but apparently I don't. Now I don't have a choice. I have to deal with him. But for real, whatever he wants, I don't want to hear it.

I get closer and see him standing on the front porch with his back to me. I walk up the path and up the front steps. He's on his cell phone. As I get closer I can hear him talking softly to someone—obviously female and obviously not Courtney. It sounds like he's making plans for tonight. No big surprise.

I step up on the porch, lean back against one of the columns and just wait. I wasn't listening to his conversation on purpose, but then again, I wasn't not listening, either. It was typical Kenneth James Lewis—cheating and stepping out. For real, I have no idea how my mom dealt with his ass for so long.

"I'm sorry, baby girl, but you know I got that thing to do," he coos softly.

I just shake my head. Did he just call one of his part-time hoochies "baby girl," the nickname he's been calling me all my life?

"Nah, baby girl, we got all weekend. Just give me a few hours to take care of this thing. I have to make a quick drop-off, okay? Then I'll come and pick you up, I promise. We'll do dinner, a club and then we'll go back to the house and I'll do you." He pauses a few seconds and laughs. "Yeah, all night long, just you and me. And wear that little red thong thing I like. You know how I like to slap that ass with my…"

Oh, my God, gross. I think I just threw up in my mouth. Twice. Okay, I seriously don't want to hear anymore, so I start down the steps to go around to the back door. I get to the last step. I can still hear him talking his old-school player bullshit, then he stops midsentence. I look back. He's looking at me. I guess he's shocked. I turn back around and keep walking.

"Baby girl," he calls out, apparently forgetting my request for him not to call me that anymore. Especially since I know that's what he calls his hoochies. "No, not you, baby girl," he says in the cell phone, then realizes his confusing mistake. "Hey, let me hit you up later. Yeah, I'll call you." He closes his cell phone fast, then calls out to me again. "Baby girl."

I turn and reluctantly go back to the front porch. I look up at him. "Who, me or her?" I question sarcastically, and glance at the phone still in his hand. He knows exactly what I'm talking about. See, I have zero respect for my dad. But it wasn't when he threw me and my mom out of the house or when he stood at her grave site acting like he was all torn up. No, it was when he and I stood watching Courtney, his current baby mama, damn near spread her legs and screw him out of everything and not say a damn word to her afterward. "Baby girl, when did you get here?"

I didn't answer his question. "Hi, Dad," I say instead.

He stares at me a few seconds. "Why didn't you tell me your grandmother's going to Georgia to visit her sister next week? Do you think you're staying in this house alone?"

"I've been in this house alone before."

"Not for seven days," he points out quickly. "Do you really think I'm gonna let you stay here by yourself all week? Pack your bags. You're coming with me to Virginia."

"What? Dad, it's no big deal. When mom was alive and went on her trips I used to be alone in the house all the time 'cause you were never there."

"Not this house and not this neighborhood."

"Dad, it's no big deal," I insist.

"This isn't up for discussion. Get in the house and pack."

Okay, see, this is what I'm talking about. He's got it into his head that after sixteen years of ignoring me, he can just step into my life now and start acting like a father. Please. "What about school next week? How am I supposed to do that?"

"I'll drive you into the city in the morning and you can meet me at my office afterward and I'll have someone take you home. Mrs. Taylor can do it," he says, opening the front door and heading into the house.

"Mrs. Taylor is your receptionist, not a driver. Besides, I have a job after school. How am I supposed to get back and forth from work?"

"A job!" He turns and yells. "When the hell did you get a job! Where is it, that pizza place again?"

My grandmother comes to the kitchen doorway instantly. She heads down the hall toward us. I don't answer him. Okay, I've heard my dad yell before, mostly when he was arguing with my mom and now with Courtney. He's never really yelled at me, not like this.

"What is all this yelling about?" my grandmother asks.

He whips around to her. "She has a job. What, nobody thought I might like to know what my daughter is doing these days? The only way I found out that she had a job and was damn near killed in a robbery was when my receptionist told me and two police officers came into my office. Nobody tells me anything anymore and I'm sick of it. I'm her father, understand? You're just her grandmother. Everything, and I mean everything, she does goes by me first, do you understand?" he demands, pointing his finger at my grandmother for emphasis.

Shit. Not a good idea. I take a step to the side and see my grandmother's eyes narrow just like my mom's used to when she was pissed off. Only my grandmother looks ten times fiercer. She looks like she's about to kick ass.

"First of all, Kenneth, don't you ever come into my home and raise your voice at me. I'm not my daughter nor one of your female friends, so your yelling doesn't move me. This is my home, you respect it. Second, you need to have a care about pointing your finger in my face. That's how fools come up short. I'm not too old that I can't kick your ass up and down this damn street. And believe me when I say, if I can't do it I know others who certainly will."

"Are you threatening me?" he asks with a smirk on his face.

"Shut up," my grandmother yells.

"Don't disrespect me in front of my daughter. I'm her—"

"I don't give a damn what you are or who you are. Don't you dare raise your voice in my home. Ever! And I'm not finished yet. Third, if you would have paid at least half the amount of attention on this child as you do on running the damn streets my daughter would still be alive and not rotting in a premature grave. You did that to her, no one else, you did!" she accuses.

Oh, shit. I didn't see this coming.

"Are you blaming me for Barbara's death? She took those damn pills and killed herself. I had nothing to do with it. I wasn't here when it happened, you were," he says.

"You knew damn well what those pills were for and what she was going through. For the last five years of her life she was suffering alone while you ran the damn street acting like some teenage jackass."

"I loved Barbara," he insists.

"Bullshit, if you loved her you never would have treated her like you did. You didn't love her and you damn sure didn't deserve her."

"You don't know me. You don't know anything about me."

"I know you're a selfish, self-centered asshole."

"Woman, you need to get up out of my face before I—"

"What? Before you what?" she interrupts him instantly. Shit, even I take a step back on that one. My grandmother's eyes and lips narrow to thin slits of rage. Her face is flushed red and her fists are balled tight on her hips. My mom was a hitter. She'd slap someone in a split second. I have no idea what my grandmother might do. I half expect her to pull out a gun and just start shooting.

"You need to change that attitude right now and know who the hell you're talking to. I'm not one of your hoochie-mamas."

Seriously, the words *hoochie-mamas* should not be coming out of my seventy-something-year-old grandmother's mouth—ever.

"You've been all up in my business for the past seventeen years and I put up with it. I'm sick of this drama with you. I don't have to put up with it anymore. I don't need you. I'll take care of Kenisha."

I laugh out loud. Oops. They both look at me. Shit.

"How the hell are you gonna take care of her when you can barely take care of yourself, let alone the family you got living in Virginia and Maryland and God knows where else."

"Whoa, back up, in Maryland?" I actually butt in, forgetting I need to be quiet. "What family in Maryland?" I ask my dad.

"Do you want to answer that question or do you want me to?"

My dad doesn't say a word. He just glares from me to my grandmother, then back at me. "Go upstairs and pack your bags, everything. You're leaving this house tonight."

Of course I don't move. "Dad, what family in Maryland?"

"Get your stuff and get your ass outside now. You're going

to Virginia," he says as he turns to the front door. "I need to get out of here."

This is so typical for my dad. He's a bailer. Whenever things get tight or uncomfortable and he can't take it anymore, he walks out. I look at my grandmother. She nods for me to go upstairs. I drop my backpack on the bottom step and head upstairs to my room. When I get to the second floor I hear the front door open and my grandmother talking again.

"No, you don't. You're not running from this. Have a seat."

I hear the door close. I don't know if my dad did what she told him or if he did his usual—walk away.

Eight

Out of the Loop—Again

kenishi_wa K Lewis
WTF? Are you friggin' kidding me? Why is it that I'm always the last person to know anything? I swear I hate being in the dark as much as I hate knowing too much.
27 Apr * Like * Comment * Share

I call Jade as soon as I get to my room. Somebody's gotta tell me something. Thank God she answers on the first ring. "Hey," she says, "I was gonna call you tonight. We need to talk about what I found out."

"Yeah, but before we do that, Jade, tell me the truth. What the hell's going on? Does my dad have another family in Maryland or what?"

"Another family? Who told you that?" she asks slowly.

Her voice was laced with caution. Right then, I know he does. Seriously, WTF is his problem. I just shake my head. Here I go again. "Grandmom and my dad were arguing and she said it."

"They were arguing about what?"

I took a deep breath. "About me not staying here at the house alone next week. I didn't tell him Grandmom's going away."

"And let me guess, now he's pissed and wants you to go back to the house in Virginia for good."

"Yeah."

"You should have told him."

"Why? For what reason? He doesn't care. My dad and I haven't spoken in almost three weeks. So, like, whenever he wants to step up and play paternal I'm just supposed to be quiet and play along. Nah, bump that shit. I'm sick of it. He's the same part-time dad he always was. He's got his thing and I've got mine. It's no big deal. I can be here in the house alone. It's only seven days."

"What do you mean? Kenisha, you're not gonna be at the house alone. I'm gonna stay there with you and commute to my classes. Grandmom and I already talked about it."

"Are you sure?" I say, a lot more hopeful and relieved than I thought I would be. "What about you being at the dorm—isn't it more convenient to be on campus?" I ask.

"Probably, but Grandmom and I already decided."

"Okay, I'll tell my dad that you're gonna be here with me next week. Hopefully that will calm him down," I say, then pause a few seconds. "Jade, did you know Grandmom blames my dad for Mom dying like that? She said that Mom was suffering."

There was a long silence on her end, and then she finally answered. "Yeah, I kinda knew or rather suspected."

"Why didn't you tell me?" I ask her.

"And say what, Kenisha? Guess what, I think our grandmother blames your father for Mom's death. How's the weather?"

"Yeah, well, I just didn't know. It surprised me when she said it. I thought she was over it. She never speaks about

Mom or wants to talk about her. Once in a while I see her looking really sad, especially when she's in the living room and looking at the family pictures on the wall."

"She's still grieving. She blames herself, too. Plus, I think Mom was actually sick when she died. That's what I was gonna call you and tell you about later. The more I look into it the more I get the feeling those hospital bills you found belonged to Mom and not to Grandmom."

"To Mom—wait, what makes you think that?"

"I have the medicine bottles I took from you that time. I did a Google search on the names of some of the prescription pills she was taking. They weren't just for her nerves like she said. They were serious pain pills."

My stomach clinches into a knot and my heart starts to beat fast. I start thinking about the dreams I've been having about her. My eyes get watery and I can feel all the emotions coming back again. I know Dr. Tubbs says to just let the emotions go, but I still can't. "What was wrong with her?" I ask just above a whisper.

"I don't know. I asked them but they won't tell me. But whatever it was I think it was serious, real serious."

"Did you know she was sick?" I ask her.

"No, I had no idea."

We both get quiet for a while. I guess we're just trying to figure all this out. I'm just sitting on the windowsill staring down at the empty street. "Can you send me the links to what you found out?"

"Yeah, sure, maybe between the two of us we can find out what was really going on."

"Jalisa's sister, Natalie, is a nurse. I think she's even at the same hospital the bills are from. I can always ask her."

"No, it's hospital policy. I don't want to get her in trouble. We'll figure something out. What are you doing tomorrow night?"

"Terrence's frat brothers are having a party. He invited me. I hear Taj is supposed to be there, too. Are you going?"

"I heard about it. I doubt it. Taj isn't exactly one of my favorite people and I know she hates my guts because of Ty."

"Oh, shit, that's right," I say, completely forgetting the drama Jade had with Taj wanting to take her fiancé, Ty.

"I'll think about going, but if Taj shows, I'm out. So do you think you can party with your big sister?"

I smile for the first time since I left school, which now seems like days ago. "Yeah, I think I can do that. Oh, my God, I forgot to tell you about my new job. Or I guess the job I was offered."

"Oh, yeah, that's right. You texted me about it, tell me."

"It's at Freeman Dance Studio. Ms. Jay asked me to help out teaching the beginner hip-hop class."

"Are you up for doing that?"

"Hell, yeah."

"Cool. Okay, listen, I have a study group in a few minutes, so I gotta go. I'll see you tomorrow."

"Wait, you didn't answer my first question. Does my dad have another family in Maryland?"

"You need to ask your dad, Kenisha."

"Jade…"

"No, you gotta ask him. I'll talk to you later," she says, then hangs up.

"Fine, I'll ask him," I say to myself. I hurry up and pack a few things into my dance bag. There's no way I'm packing to leave for good. I just get what I need for dance and tonight and that's all. I go downstairs and as soon as I get to the bottom landing I hear it—nothing. It's quiet, too quiet. I walk into the living room. I look for my grandmother, but she's not there. I see my dad standing to the side looking at the pictures on the wall. One is a photo of my mom. I stand there for a few minutes and watch him staring at it. He's not smiling or sad, he's just standing there staring. I wonder what's going through his mind.

After a while I speak. "Dad, can we talk?" I say. He turns to me. His eyes are glazed over like he's about to cry.

"Sit down," he says. I do. He walks over to the fireplace. "Imagine my surprise when I walk in here this afternoon and your grandmother tells me she'll be away all next week. I had no idea she's going to visit her sister. You didn't tell me."

This is seriously not what I want to talk to him about right now. "We haven't been talking to each other for a while."

"I've called and texted you."

I didn't say anything. What he said wasn't exactly true. Yeah, yesterday and today he did call and text me, but what about the past three weeks? I know I don't want to get into all that with him, so I just agree. "I know."

"There's no way you're staying in this house alone for a week. No way," he says.

"I'm not going to be alone. Jade's staying here with me. She's gonna commute to school instead of staying in the dorm."

"The two of you in this neighborhood, no, the house has already been broken into."

"Yeah, but since then, Grandmom had the new security system installed. Now it's like living in Fort Knox. It's set up so that we have to code into the system to get in and also once we're inside. So we're always safe since security is on all the windows and doors."

"Why didn't you tell me your grandmother is going to Georgia for a week?"

I shrug. "I didn't run and tell you because I guess I figured it didn't matter to you. *I* didn't matter to you. You already have another baby girl, so…"

"Kenisha." He softens instantly. "I'm your father. I'm always going to be your father no matter what happens in my life or between us. Of course it matters to me, *you* matter to me. I love you," he says.

I purposely don't respond. It's time to change the subject to what I want to talk about. "Dad, do you have another family in Maryland?"

He looks me right in the eyes and avoids the question. "Tell me about this new job of yours," he says.

Of course he's blocking. I knew he would. It's what he does. "The job's at Freeman Dance Studio. Ms. Jay, the owner, offered it to me yesterday. She was supposed to talk to Grandmom this morning about it. If Grandmom approves of the hours I can do it."

He shook his head. "No, if she wants you to work for her, then she needs to talk to me, not your grandmother," he says. "When she does that, we'll go from there. Are you packed?"

"I just have my dance bag packed," I say. He looks at me. "I'm supposed to meet Jalisa and Diamond at Freeman for practice today. Can I please go and then have them drop me off at the house in Virginia instead of leaving with you now?" He looks at me a few seconds as if he's assessing whether or not I'm lying. Since I wasn't, I was cool.

"All right, I want you in the house by nine o'clock," he says, then stands and turns to leave.

"Dad, practice isn't even over until nine," I complain.

"Fine, leave early. Nine o'clock," he repeats more firmly with his hand on the front doorknob. As soon as he opens it there's a beeping sound. I quickly reset the alarm before it sounds for real.

"That's it, huh?"

"Yes, it has both a silent and audio alarm. The main feed is connected to the main system at the security company plus to the police, fire and emergency services system. So, what about it?" I ask.

He's looking at the system, then turns to me. "What about what?"

"Me staying here with Jade next week. Is it okay? Please."

He relents. "Fine, I'll call Jade and tell her you're grounded and have a curfew. And tonight make sure you're at the house by nine o'clock," he insisted.

"Are you gonna be home?"

He gives me that look. We both know he won't be. And now we both know I won't, either. He leaves right after that, so I lock the door behind him and go into the kitchen. My grandmother is in there. I sit down at the table across from her. "I'm sorry about that, Grandmom. I guess I should have told him about your visiting your sister and not being here next week."

She nods her head, agreeing. "Yes, you should have."

"I just didn't think it mattered to him what I did."

"He's your father, Kenisha. It matters. He may not always appear to show it the way you think he should, but it matters."

"Does he have another family in Maryland like you said?"

"I shouldn't have suggested that," she says.

"Does he?"

"You need to ask him about that."

"I did. He changed the subject."

"Well, then, I will, too. Are you going to dance class today?"

"Yes, then I'm supposed to go to the house right after. Jalisa and Diamond can give me a ride. Are you still going to bingo tonight?"

She glances at her watch. "Yes, Grace and Edith should be here soon. Lord, I have so much to do still."

"I can stay and help if you want."

"No, no, you go on to class. I'll be fine."

"Well, since you're leaving tomorrow morning, I guess this is it," I say, smiling. "Have a great time, Grandmom. Don't worry about the house. I promise not to have too many wild parties while you're gone."

"Now you know I know better than that since you don't want me coming home early."

"I know. I'm just joking. Don't worry, I got this."

She chuckled, shaking her head. "Lord, child, you sound just like your mother saying that. 'I got this.'"

"Can I ask you something?" I ask. She nods. "You used to talk about Mom all the time, but now you don't any-more, why?"

"I don't know. I guess perhaps it hurts too much know-ing that my child is gone before me. That's not supposed to happen. A parent is never supposed to bury their child."

"I dream about her a lot. In the dream we're together and then we get separated and I have to watch her go away."

"Our dreams are a way of helping us sort through our feeling and our pain. You're making sense out of all this."

"All those pills Mom was taking before she died… I'm thinking now they were more than just for her nerves like she said. Was she sick?"

My grandmother looks at me sadly, then reaches out and covers my hand with hers. She pats it gently. "None of that matters anymore, sweetie. There's no pain. She's at rest now."

"I understand, but I still need to know. What was wrong with her?" I ask, holding my breath, not sure I'm ready to hear the answer. Still, I want to know. I need to know. But a part of me is afraid. I watch her closely. She takes a deep breath and shakes her head slowly while exhaling. All this and she still doesn't speak. "Grandmom, it's okay. You can tell me." Just as she opens her mouth the doorbell rings. She smiles, pats my hand a couple more times and then stands and walks away. I don't know if she was going to tell me or not. I guess I won't know now.

A few minutes later she calls to tell me she's on her way to bingo. I get up and go to the front door. I see two of her friends standing in the foyer. "Hi, Ms. Edith, Hi, Ms. Grace."

"Good Lord, look at you, Kenisha. If I didn't know any better I'd say I was standing here looking at your mother. Doesn't she look just like Barbara?" Ms. Edith says.

Ms. Grace nods, agreeing. "Sure 'nuff, just like her. Jade, too. Good Lord, these girls are growing up so fast. You know that makes you old, Edith."

They both laugh while I just smile. At about seventy-five years old, they still act like they're twenty-two. They dress young, wear tons of makeup and dye their hair blond so the gray won't show as much. They text on their cell phones, watch only Blu-ray movies and know all the latest music and dance steps. Sometimes I wish my grandmother would act more like them. And then again, maybe not.

"All right, let's get this show on the road. I have just about enough time to win super-bingo, finish packing my clothes for the trip and then save the world from falling asteroids," my grandmom jokes.

Now everybody laughs. My grandmother opens her arms and smiles at me. I go to her. This is the last time I'll see her for a while. "Have a good time, Grandmom, and don't forget to call me or text me."

"I will. Now you know the rules. No boys, no parties, no drama. I know you'll be just fine," she says, then hugs and kisses my cheek.

"I will. Have a good time tonight and have a good trip."

We hug again, but this time it feels like neither one of us wants to ever let go. But we finally do. She leaves and I stand on the porch watching them pile into Ms. Edith's old 1990 Cadillac Seville. She waves from the passenger seat and I wave back. A few minutes later I go back up to my room. I grab my cell and text a message, telling my girls, Jalisa and Diamond, I'm on my way to Freeman. They respond that they're on the way, too. I know it's gonna take them a lot longer since they live in Virginia and I live here in D.C. Still, I grab three bottles of water from the refrigerator and some cookies and head to the front door. I see my backpack on the upstairs landing and decide to take it up to my room when I get back home later. I still have to pack a few things for the weekend, including something to wear to the party with my lawnmower guy.

As soon as I get outside and start walking to Freeman, I see Li'l T sitting on somebody's steps with a few other guys. I go over to him. He sees me, gets up and meets me halfway. "Did you take that down yet?"

"No, not yet," he says.

I look at him fiercely. "Do you think I'm playing with you? This isn't a joke. I don't want that up."

"What's the big deal? Most girls would love to have this kind of attention on YouTube. Damn, girl, it's not like it's something embarrassing. You look good up there."

"That's not the point, and I'm not most girls."

"Okay, okay, but I gotta hold up for a minute. I gotta wait until I catch up with my cousin."

I roll my eyes. "What is your problem? Just take it down."

"I don't have my flat pad anymore."

"Where is it?" I ask.

"Like I said, I gotta catch up with my cousin."

I shake my head and just turn and walk away. I can't believe how crazy this is getting. As soon as I get to Freeman, I head straight to the office. Ms. Jay is there and she looks a lot better than she did yesterday. "Hi, Ms. Jay," I say.

"Hi, Kenisha," she says. "How are you today?"

"I'm okay. Can we use one of the rooms upstairs today?"

She shakes her head. "We mopped the floors and cleaned up all morning, but I still have a ways to go," she says, then goes in her drawer and pulls out the auditorium key like before. "Here, you can use the auditorium again. Just remember to—"

"I know," I say as I take the key from her, "turn off the lights and lock the music cage and auditorium doors when we're done. I will. Thank you."

"Sure. Oh, I tried speaking with your grandmother earlier, but we've been playing phone tag all day. Is she home now?"

"No, and she'll be away all next week starting tomorrow morning. But you can speak with my dad. Here's his cell phone number," I say, quickly scribbling the number on a piece of paper.

She nods. "Okay, this will work. Oh," she says, smiling broadly, "I was sent a YouTube link this morning. It was of you dancing. You looked wonderful. Is that an original piece?"

"Yes, it's a song I started writing right after my mom died. It doesn't have a name yet. Actually, it wasn't supposed to be seen, but one of the guys I know taped it and put it up."

"It's beautiful and your dancing is stunning in the piece. I'm not surprised, of course. You, Jalisa and Diamond have always excelled. You three are the best students I've had in a long time."

"Thanks, Ms. Jay."

"Also, Kenisha, I've been thinking about what you suggested yesterday. I think a dance fundraiser is a great idea. I'm gonna do it."

"Really? Cool, 'cause I was telling Jalisa and Diamond about the fundraiser last night and we had a lot of ideas we'd like to talk to you about," I say just as the office phone rings.

"That'll work. I have two classes to teach right now, so we can talk in an hour or so."

"Okay, we'll be in the auditorium when you're ready."

She answers the phone, and I leave and head upstairs instead of going to the auditorium to my favorite place. I open the door and look around. It's the first time I've seen it since the rains. The floor is still all spotted and there are buckets and wet towels everywhere. The tiles on the ceiling are hanging heavy and some are even gone and sitting against the back wall. I walk past all that to the windowsill.

I sit down, turn on my iPhone, plug in my earbuds and then open my recipe book. It's only been a few months since my grandmother suggested I start one and already it's almost full. Of course I have other things in it and not just recipes.

Mostly I have my thoughts and ideas and even a few songs I wrote. I start thinking about how my life is finally getting back to normal, or as normal as it can be given all the drama still going on around me. For real, it's like everybody I know is dealing with some kind of craziness. My grandmother has these massive hospital bills that she refuses to talk about. My sister, Jade, and her on-again, off-again fiancé, Ty, are still going through their thing about him stepping out on her. My girls, Jalisa and Diamond, are stressing about college and, of course, guys.

And then there's my lawnmower guy, Terrence. I don't really know what to say about him. I guess he's okay for right now. Or rather we're okay for right now. At least he's talking to me again. But his old girlfriend, Gia, is still hanging around trying to cause trouble. I know she's trying to get back in with him, but seriously, that's definitely not about to happen. At least I hope not. He says they're just old friends. I don't know, maybe they are. What I do know is that he's there. She's there and I'm here.

I look down at the street below while sitting in my perch above it all. The top floor in one of the private dance studios is the perfect place to just sit, think and write in my recipe book. I check to see if Jalisa and Diamond are coming. I don't see them. All I see is some guys hanging on the corner. One of them is Li'l T. I can tell by the way he's jumping around. I shake my head. I think I'm gonna have to get serious with him. I'm not sure what I'm gonna do, but I'm definitely gonna do something.

Then I think I see Diamond's mom's car drive up, but it's not. That car keeps going. They're probably still in Virginia. My music pauses because there's a text message coming in. I look at my cell phone and see it's from Jalisa.

We're almost there, she says.

Hurry up. I feel like dancing, I text back.

Double ditto!

Just then I see a shadow on the floor. I look up and see Troy's little sister standing in the doorway. I have no idea how long she's been there. I pull an earbud out. "Hey, Hannah, are you lost?"

"No," she says slightly sulky, then walks over and peeks out the window near where I'm sitting and then looks at me. "You go to school with my brother, Troy, right?"

I nod. I have no idea where she's going with this.

"I think he likes you," she says.

"Really," I say.

"Do you like him?"

"I don't really know him, but he's okay as a friend, I guess."

"No, I mean do you like him for a boyfriend. He likes you."

"But he knows I already have a boyfriend."

"Where is he, at Penn Hall, too?"

"No, he's in college. He goes to Howard University," I say. Hannah nods, then it looks like she wants to say something more, but she doesn't. She just stares out the window again.

"Aren't you supposed to be in dance class now?" I ask her.

She shrugs. "Can you really do all that stuff you did in the YouTube video?"

"Yeah, I can," I say. "Why?"

"I was just wondering," she says, then pauses. "How long did it take to learn all that?"

"A long time—I've been dancing since I was four, remember?"

"I don't get what they're doing," she says.

"What do you mean, in dance class?"

She shrugs again. "Yeah, in my hip-hop class. I can't catch on 'cause they do it too fast. I left. I like it better when you teach class. You do it step by step and I get it then."

"Show me what you think it looks like they're doing. Maybe I can help and walk you through it slower. Do you know what song you're dancing to? I probably have it. I have about three thousand songs on this thing." She tells me. I pull the other earbud out of my ear and find the song. I turn the volume up all the way. The song comes on and she starts dancing. I watch her. She's stiff and kinda uncoordinated.

"Okay, I remember that routine," I say, then stand next to her. "Let's start from the beginning and take it slowly." We start dancing and I'm giving her hints and tips on how to make her body move in a more hip-hop style. After a while she looks a lot better. It's obvious she's getting it. We're right in the middle of doing the routine again when the music cuts off. "Hold on, I have a text message," I say, then check the small screen.

K, where are you? Jalisa texts.

Third floor—Studio A, I respond.

We're looking for a place to park. We'll be there in a few minutes.

Okay, I say.

"Okay, let's try it one more time," I say to Hannah.

"Was that your boyfriend?"

"No, my girls—they dance here, too."

"You mean the ones in the picture with you?"

"Yeah, come on, from the top."

"Would you come to my birthday party next Saturday?" she blurts out quickly. "It's gonna be fun, I promise."

Wow, didn't expect that. It's been a long time since I got invited to a for-real kid's birthday party. "Um, I don't know."

"I know you're old and stuff and you probably have other things to do, but if you can…"

"I'll tell you what. If I can, I will. But I'll definitely get you a gift either way. What do you want?"

She smiles easily and her eyes sparkle. "I want to dance like you."

"Well, then, I guess we'd better get started. Ready?" I ask. She nods. I turn the music back on. We do the routine once more and this time she's really good. Just as we end I hear laughter and talking down the hallway. I already know who it is—Jalisa and Diamond.

NINE

Life Is Good!

kenishi_wa K Lewis
I've learned to live by my actions and deal with the consequences. I take the bad with the good and deal with whatever comes my way. Right now it's all good.
27 Apr * Like * Comment * Share

A few seconds later the studio door bursts open and Jalisa and Diamond come in. They're laughing and talking loud and boisterous. "Hey." "We're here," they say in unison.

"Hey," I say, happy to see them.

"There she is, the download superstar herself," Jalisa adds, laughing loudly.

"No way, she's our download diva," Diamond jokes.

"See, y'all need to stop with all that," I say, knowing they're just playing with me.

"Okay, I gotta go to class now, thanks for helping me," Hannah says, then looks at Jalisa and Diamond as she walks out.

"Wait a minute, Hannah," I say. She turns around. "I want you to meet my friends. This is Jalisa Saunders and Diamond Riggs. Ladies, this is Hannah Carson."

"Hi," they all say.

"Thanks again for helping me," she says, then gets to the studio door and turns around. "Troy really likes you. You should get rid of your boyfriend and hang out with him. He's not as bad as he tries to act." She leaves quickly.

Jalisa and Diamond look at each other, then at me. "What's that about?" Jalisa asks quietly.

"Hannah, she goes to class here. I was helping her with her hip-hop moves. She's a little stiff. She needs to loosen up."

"Who's Troy?" Diamond asks.

I just shake my head. "He goes to Penn Hall. Y'all met him at LaVon's party before. That's his little sister—" I glance back at the door "—I guess we're best buds now." They turn and look, too. Then I start smiling again. "It's good to see y'all."

"You, too," Diamond says.

"Hey," Jalisa says again, much louder this time.

"Hey," I repeat happily. Diamond repeats it, too. We hug and start talking all at once. It's been almost two and a half weeks since we've seen one another. Sure, we talk on the phone, video, Skype, text and tweet constantly, but seeing one another is always the best.

"Oh, my God, girl, we saw you on YouTube," Diamond adds excitedly.

"Everybody did. The whole school is talking about you."

"Oh, my God, yeah, they're sharing it everywhere and saying you're the next Taj—it's so cool. The video's, like, going viral in Hazelhurst and everywhere else."

"Oh, and you would not believe what else. Your girl Chili is about to lose her friggin' mind 'cause you're getting all the attention. She is seriously hating on you now, girl."

"When'd you upload it?"

"I didn't," I say. "Li'l T did. He videoed me yesterday while I was practicing downstairs in the auditorium. I didn't even know he did it until after everyone started talking about seeing it. I told him not to video me, but he did anyway. All I know now is that if he doesn't take it down I'm gonna strangle him."

They laugh. "Eew, look at this studio," Jalisa says, looking around and seeing the messed-up ceiling and floor. "I thought you were exaggerating, but you were right. It looks horrible. The leaking roof did all this?"

I nod. Diamond starts looking around, then she sniffs and makes a face. "What's that smell? A dead animal?"

"No, I think it might be the ceiling tiles getting all moldy or something like that."

"We seriously cannot practice here."

"I know. Ms. Jay already gave me the key to the auditorium. We can go down to the stage." I get up and we all walk downstairs to the first floor. They keep complaining about what the building looks like now since they haven't been here in a few weeks. When we get to the auditorium I unlock the door and turn on the lights. They flicker a few seconds, then finally come on full wattage. All of the sudden it's super bright like daylight. We look around.

"Oh, my God, y'all remember when we used to do our recitals in here years ago?" Jalisa says.

"Oh, man, those were crazy. I hated doing them. I was always petrified that I'd mess up and fall on my face," Diamond says.

"Not me. I loved them," Jalisa says.

"Hey, y'all remember when I broke my toe and didn't tell?"

"Oh, yeah, I remember. It was about to turn blue and

we made you tell Ms. Jay and she took you directly to the hospital. Your mom was so pissed at you for not saying anything and you were pissed at us for telling."

"Yeah, 'cause I didn't want to lose my place in the spring recital. Do you believe how crazy that sounds now? How old were we then?"

"I think we were ten or eleven, something like that."

I start walking down toward the stage. "Come on, y'all, are we gonna stand around here talking all day or are we gonna dance?"

"Dance," we all yell in unison, then run down to the stage. We drop our stuff backstage, then Diamond and Jalisa go to the front. I unlock the music cage and plug my cell phone into the dock. I pick a bunch of hip-hop, rock and rap songs. The music starts. We change to wear crop-top tees, tanks and fishnet tops, dance sweatpants, booty shorts and leggings, cargo shorts, fedoras and caps and then we go back on stage to stretch.

Jalisa puts on strap dance heels with leg warmers, I wear dance sneaks and sweats and Diamond wears pointe ballet shoes laced up her ankle. Three styles of dance are represented and for the next hour and a half we interchange and do it all. We dance, play, laugh, talk, joke and then dance some more. After a while people start coming in and out of the auditorium, but we don't pay much attention to them. We're having too much fun being together and dancing.

The rhythm goes hard. We're instantly energized. We start to dance our routine, something we've been working on for a few weeks. We said that when it's good enough we're gonna show it to Gayle Harmon, the choreographer. We try out some new stuff Diamond came up with. Jalisa and I both add on to it. It's really starting to look good.

Seriously, it's really hot. Some of the dance instructors come in to see us, including Ms. Jay.

They're cheering and applauding by the time we really get into it. We're all three doing the same step, but to a different downbeat, with different timing and different dance styles—hip-hop, ballet and jazz. The visual is different and exciting. When the music ends it looks like we have half the school in the auditorium with us. They're applauding and cheering and we're bowing and laughing. I usually don't like the whole in-front-of-a-crowd audience-recital thing, but this time I really like the attention. It feels great.

So we leave about two hours later. It's dark outside now and I'm happy Diamond drove her car. We decide to stop at Giorgio's pizza place before home. This is the first time I've been in there since the robbery. And even though it's been months, it still feels strange. Neither Sierra nor Ursula are here. They never caught all the guys involved in the robbery, so now I'm sitting looking around and thinking it could be anybody here right now. That gives me the creeps. We eat a slice, and then share a cookie like we always do.

"So what are y'all doing tomorrow night?" I ask.

"Nothing, why?" Jalisa says.

"I have to work until eight, but after that I'm free," Diamond adds.

"Cool, Terrence told me about this party tomorrow night. It's at one of his frat brothers' houses. It's supposed to be nice, and Taj is supposed to show up. Do you want to come?"

"Where is it?"

"It's in Virginia. I don't know where exactly, but he said it's not too far from where my dad lives, so it's gotta be in the neighborhood someplace. He's driving. Want to come?"

"Cool, sounds good. I want to go."

"Yeah, me, too. I'm in," Diamond says, munching on the last of her cookie.

We start talking about other stuff and just as the conversation turns to Darien being back, he walks in the door. I'm facing that way, so I see him and he sees me. Shit. He walks over to our table and looks down at me. "Kenisha."

I don't say anything. He leans down close to my ear and whispers so no one else can hear. "Miss me?" His hot breath tickles my neck, but I still don't say anything. I just grimace and cringe away, looking at my girls sitting across the booth from me. "Do you really think we're over? Nah, we have unfinished business," he says, then leans up and walks away. It feels like my skin crawls.

He's goes to the other side of the room, but I can still feel his body next to me and his hot breath on my neck. It's creepy.

Both Jalisa and Diamond stare, then lean over looking at me. "Are you okay? Do you want me to call the police?" Diamond asks.

"What'd he say?" Jalisa also asks. "Did he threaten you?"

"I gotta go now," I whisper.

"Yeah, let's go," Jalisa says, nodding.

"Come on, it's getting late anyway. I need to get my mom's car back. I'll give you a ride to your grandma's house."

"I only need to pick up a few things for the weekend and then we can go to Virginia. My dad's on one of his parental rampages. He wants me in the house by nine o'clock."

Jalisa and Diamond look at each other. It was already close to nine-thirty. "I think you're gonna be late," Jalisa says.

"It doesn't matter. He's not gonna be home anyway. I heard him making plans for tonight with one of his skanks."

"All right, let's go and get your stuff," Jalisa says.

We get up and leave. I spare one quick glance in Darien's direction as we walk to the door. He's sitting in a booth with another guy and he's staring right at me. I look away, but not before I see him lick and then pucker his lips to blow me a kiss. Gross. My stomach turns and not in a good way.

We pile into the car and head to my grandmother's house. It's just around the corner and down a couple of blocks, so we get there quickly. I look up and see the timed lights are on and I know my grandmother's still at bingo with her friends. If she was back her bedroom light would be on, too. When we get to my bedroom, Jalisa and Diamond crash on my bed while I start packing.

I only gather enough for the weekend 'cause I know I'm gonna be able to talk my father into letting me come back here and stay with Jade while Grandmom's out of town. I leave a note and then we head out. As we drive through the neighborhood to get to Virginia, I start thinking about the craziness that's happened in the past few months.

If anyone would have told me a year ago that I'd be living in D.C. with my grandmother and worrying about jobs, money and bills, I would have thought they were nuts. But here I am. This is definitely not how I always thought my life would be like. But I guess nobody thinks that.

So a while later Diamond drops me off and as soon I get in the house I see that my dad's car isn't there. No big surprise. I have a key now, so I walk in the front door. It's quiet, so I decide to liven things up. I call out and an instant later the boys charge me. "Kenisha's home, Kenisha's home," they yell and scream in the singsong way they do.

I just start laughing and smiling. Jr. and Jason always crack me up. They're like mini-me's on a serious five-energy-drink high. They're always jumping and dancing, always in trouble and always loving it. Out of everything that has gone on in our connected lives, they are the innocents. My dad, Courtney, my mom, me—we all make our decisions. They don't have a choice right now.

"Hey, munchkin, hey, lollipop kid," I say, giving the boys another new nickname like I always do. This one from *The Wizard of Oz* movie we watched the last time I was here. I bend down and grab them each up in my arms and hug them fiercely. "Miss me?"

They start jumping, dancing and yelling my name again. I join in the dance and we're all laughing and having a good time. Then they start screaming, laughing and flapping their arms, pretending to be the winged monkeys. I can't help but crack up. They are so funny.

At first, when we watched the movie, I thought they'd be scared, so every time the wicked witch and the monkeys came out I laughed. They laughed, too. Then they started flying around my bedroom just like they're doing now. I love being a big sister.

"What the hell is all that noise going on down there? Stop it. I told y'all to get your asses in bed. I have a headache."

The boys and I look up the staircase. Not seeing Courtney is almost as bad as seeing her when she screams and yells like that. I start humming the Wicked Witch of the West theme and they get even wilder, flapping and flying and laughing hysterically. So the more Courtney yells the louder we get, me humming and them laughing. Then she appears at the top of the stairs. Her long weaved-in hair is all over the place and she's dressed in a tight miniskirt and crop top that, at sixteen, I wouldn't even consider wearing. She's trying hard to look young to keep my dad. But she comes off just pathetic.

After the stupid stunt she pulled with her lawyer, she's doing everything she can to stay in good with him. That means she's not bitching about money all day long anymore. It wouldn't matter, anyway, because apparently my dad has completely cut her off. He's paying everything in the house and she has absolutely no say. Seriously, it was a stupid thing to do and now she's paying for it.

"Shut up," she screams again as she gets closer.

The sudden sight of her makes the boys scream and hide behind me. It is so funny and I swear I didn't make them do this. So now I can't stop laughing and they start laughing and Courtney comes down the stairs looking even more crazy, if that's even possible, and then she gets right in my face with her eyes blaring red. Bad idea.

"I am so sick of you messing with my children. As soon as you walk your ass in the door they start acting like this. They never do this when you're not here."

"Then I guess I'd better visit more often," I say.

She glares at me, and if I didn't know any better I'd say she was a half second away from smacking me like I smacked her the first time we met, but she knows better. I have so much anger when it comes to her that once I start I don't think I'll ever stop kicking her ass. So we just glare at each other. After a while the boys start peeking out from behind me, giggling. They think this is all part of the *Wizard of Oz* thing—the good witch verses the Wicked Witch of the West.

"I hope you didn't bring that damn movie back in this house. I told your father and he agrees with me," she states proudly, like it's never happened before. Oh, right, it never has. LOL.

"Yeah! Yeah! Yeah! It's movie time. Can we see the movie again? Please, please, please. Wizard of Obs! Wizard of Obs! Can we, can we, can we? Please, please, please." Jr. and Jason start jumping and chanting over and over again.

Courtney looks at them fiercely. "Would y'all please shut that noise up. I told you I have a headache." Then she turns back to me. "Don't you dare let them watch that movie again."

"Actually, Courtney, I have another movie for them to watch. It's called *Jaws*." Her eyes immediately bulge open. So of course I start singing the two-note theme. The boys join in instantly while laughing. They're so cute.

"Stop. Shut up!" Courtney screams.

They do and just stand at my side holding my hands. The thing is I know she would never lay a hand on them and she knows I know it. The repercussions would be too great. Her ass would get kicked out of the house she loves so much and she'd have nothing. There's no way she'd risk that even to save her sanity. She loves this life too much, even if she's still only on the fringes of it.

"Look, Kenisha," she begins quietly, "we don't get along, that's fine. We're never gonna get along. I get it and that's fine, too. But you have to respect me in my house, do you understand me?"

I just smile. Courtney trying to come off all mature just isn't working. I have to smack her down. But I don't use my fists; verbally works so much better. "Oh, you mean like you respected my mother in our house? Do you understand me?"

She doesn't say anything. We just stare at each other. She

knows this is never going to end between us. The harder she pushes, the harder I push back. And now that I have the boys on my side she has nothing. She purposely came after my mother and got us kicked out. Now I'm purposely coming after her. But seriously, I don't want her kicked out of the house like she did us. My little brothers need a nice neighborhood to grow up in and this is it. And besides, it's way too much fun with her being here.

"Go to bed," she snarls between gritted teeth. The boys don't move. They stay at my side still. "I said go to bed," she repeats. They still don't move. She cocks her head to the side. "I'm gonna count to ten and you had better be moving." She starts counting, but slows when she gets to six 'cause it's obvious they're not moving until I do. "Seven. Eight…"

All of the sudden I see it in her eyes. It's only there for a split second, but it is there—a plea for compliance. I swear I don't know why I'm relenting and being nice, but whatever… "Come on, guys," I say to them. We start going upstairs. At first we're quiet and then I start, unable to resist. "Lions and tigers and bears, oh, my…" They immediately start repeating it and I say the "oh, my" part. As we chant the words we move faster and faster until we're almost running up the stairs. By the time we get to the top step they're happily laughing their crazy little heads off.

Of course I'm not going to let the boys watch *Jaws*. That's way over the top. We're probably gonna watch *Monsters, Inc.* for the hundredth time, but she doesn't have to know that. I glance back down the stairs as the boys run to my bedroom. Courtney is sitting on the steps with her head on her knees crying. I don't know why I don't feel sorry for her. I just don't. I guess I'm still not that nice.

ten

Party Over Here

kenishi_wa K Lewis
It's been a long time since I let myself relax and have a good time. I've been stressed out, beat down and worn out for too damn long. It's time to change all that.
28 Apr * Like * Comment * Share

TERRENCE takes my hand and glances at me as he turns the corner. It's dark in the car, but I can still see his eyes. He's smiling and his eyes kinda crinkle and spark. It feels so good being out with him like this. We go out sometimes to the movies or to neighborhood parties, but mostly we just hang at the mall or at my dad's or grandmother's house. But tonight is special. Tonight I get to hang with his friends.

My girls are in the backseat talking and laughing. They're really excited. It's our first *real* frat college party. We've gone to supposed-to-be college parties before, but they were just dull wannabes. There the guys were either drunk or high and trying to get us drunk or high just to get in our pants. So I don't count them. But tonight is the real thing. It's like stepping out in society. This is our time.

I look down at the outfit I chose to wear. It's hot and just about sexy without being over the top. It's definitely too tame for Courtney, who was screaming her head off when I left. She threatened to tell my father, who has yet to show his face, I was going out. I had to laugh. She hasn't heard from him since I got there last night. Any bit of self-respect would have her walking out on him, but I can't really talk since my mom never did, either… Whatever.

I guess my mood kinda changes 'cause Terrence squeezes my hand gently and speaks softly so that only I can hear him. "Hey, you okay over there?"

I nod. "Yes, I'm great."

"Did I tell you that you look good tonight, girl? I don't want to have throw-down with any of my brothers up in there trying to get with you."

I smile. "Don't worry, you got me." I squeeze his hand gently. He nods and now I just can't stop smiling.

He turns a corner and cars are already lining up along the streets. "All right, here we go. Are you ready for this?" Terrence asks. I nod, then turn and look in the backseat. Jalisa and Diamond are smiling like crazy. We nod our heads excitedly. "All right, let's do this," he says as he pulls into a parking space. We get out and walk down the block and around the corner. The houses are massive here, nowhere near the size of my old neighborhood. It's a few miles from my dad's house, but not too far from where LaVon, my ex-boyfriend, lives. It's one of those minimansions that looks small on the outside, but is probably huge on the inside. "Here it is," Terrence says.

We walk up the long driveway path and as soon we get to the open front porch there are about six guys standing there. They greet Terrence and do this handshake kinda thing that I don't recognize, then he introduces me and my girls. A couple of the guys are instantly on Jalisa and Diamond, then Terrence steps in. "Yo, my brothers, respect," he says, and tells them they're here with him. They nod and take a step back.

So we walk to the front door and, okay, first of all there's no other way to say it—the party is slammin'. Seriously, as soon as we walk into the house, I'm like, oh, my God, you gotta be kidding me. The music is blaring loud and the place is packed. It looks like just about all of Howard University showed up and that's definitely major.

We start walking around the house going to the different rooms. It's got everything—game room, heated pool, solarium, family room, exercise room, theater—and those are just the rooms I saw. There are people all over the place. Then after a while we split up. Terrence goes to talk with some of his friends and Jalisa, Diamond and I hang out by the dance floor.

We're laughing and talking and having a great time. Terrence comes over, bringing a couple of guys from his dorm and we all start dancing. Of course we're all over the place. People are stepping back and giving us the floor. Terrence and his two friends are smiling and joining in but they know they can't keep up with us. We start doing one of the routines we've practiced. It's pure hip-hop and it's really hot. Some pull out their cell phones and start taping us. We don't really care, 'cause we're having too much fun.

Then a slow song comes on and Terrence takes my hand. He pulls me farther to the dance floor. We stand there a few seconds and then he leans down and kisses my lips as he wraps his arms around my waist. I move closer and our bodies touch. After the kiss we just stand there looking at each other. "You look good dancing, girl. Got me all impressed with you."

"You've seen me dance before."

"Yeah, but not like all that," he says, then looks around. "I think there are a few guys still watching you and licking their chops. I think you got their attention."

I reach up and turn his face back to me. "You are the only guy whose attention I want."

He smiles and nods. "A'ight, I guess I can handle that."

"Good." I lean up and kiss him again. Then all of the sudden it starts to get noisy and people leave and head to the front of the house. "What is it, a fight or something?"

"I don't know," he says. We stop dancing. He takes my hand and I follow him to see what's going on. There's a mad rush to the front door. We go along to find out what all the drama is about. As soon as we get to the front porch I see Jalisa and Diamond already standing there. "Hey, what's going on?" I ask them.

"Somebody said Taj's whip just pulled up," Jalisa says.

"For real," I say.

"I don't know. I can't see," Diamond says.

"Me, either," Jalisa adds.

I lean on Terrence and step up on my toes to see if I can spot her. I can't. It's too dark and there're too many people in front of us. Then there's a loud cheer and people start dancing and applauding. Taj's latest song starts playing. I look around. The music is coming from the outside speakers. "Come on," Terrence says, then grabs my hand and pulls me. "Get your girls." I grab Jalisa and she grabs Diamond. He leads us down the front lawn and around to the side. When he stops we're right up front and we can see everything perfectly.

More lights turn on and now we can really see what's happening. Taj steps up to perform and the crowd goes wild.

"Oh, my God, it is her," Diamond says.

"Look at her," Jalisa says, laughing. "What is she wearing?"

"Oh, my God, I don't know. I can't believe we're seeing this."

"Damn, she is still buck wild."

She had on fraternity colors—a long black wig with gold streaks, a too-tight gold sequined bra barely holding her extra-large boobs, black shorts that are spandex tight and barely covering her up and crazy high-heel stilettos. I know I mess with Courtney about her trashy clothes, but damn, Taj is way, way over the top even for an entertainer.

Terrence and a few of his buddies start hollering and it's like everybody that was inside the house is now outside on the front lawn watching the miniconcert. We're dancing and singing. The place is a madhouse and we're having a blast.

So then she starts grinding and shaking her ass all over the place and acting like she's making out on the car's top. I'm watching with my mouth wide-open. I seriously can't believe she's doing all this at a private neighborhood party. Then another song mixes in and the tempo changes. She starts walking through the crowd.

Taj comes to where we're dancing and playing around. She tries to match our steps, but can't. Everybody sees that she's not as good as we are. She starts talking about how well we dance and everybody starts applauding 'cause most of them saw us dancing inside. Now she tries to make it look like we're part of her group because people start checking us out and not her.

The microphone is loud and she's all sweaty. But for real I can't believe how tiny and skinny she is. Up close she looks like a little kid dressed for Halloween. Then she sees Terrence and goes right over to him. She sings to him and starts unbuttoning his shirt and rubbing her hands all over his chest. Then she takes his hand and rubs it all down the front of her. His boys are going wild.

She smiles and pulls him back to where she was singing on top of the car. She backs Terrence up against it and I swear my jaw just drops. I can't believe she's doing this right in front of me, in front of everybody. Okay, I get that she has no idea that he's with somebody—me—but damn, girl. A little respect for yourself, please.

His boys are all hollering for him, but thankfully he's looking too embarrassed to be up there with her. I guess other guys would be right in there eating all the attention up. Terrence isn't. He tries to walk away but she stops him and talks about him being shy and how she always had a crush on him when she was around the way, but that he always saw her as just a kid. "Well, T, do I look like a kid now," she says, and grinds her body against his on the beat of her song. "Do I feel like a kid now?" The guys in the audience go wild.

There's no stopping the craziness now. He comes back over to me, shaking his head. All his friends are slapping his back, bumping his shoulder and shaking his hand as Taj continues her performance. But no matter what she was singing or where she was in the crowd, she always had her eye on us. By us, I mean Terrence.

Everybody's hanging out and having a good time. Then after a while we see red and blue lights flashing down the street. Everyone knows it's only a matter of time before the police show up. They always do. They tell Terrence's friend that his party is gonna have to go back inside the house and quiet down some. We comply. Some go inside while others go back to their cars and leave.

Now inside it's like half the people there and it feels a lot better. We go to the game room. Terrence starts playing pool with some guys and me and my girls are standing around watching, plus talking to some other girls about college life.

About a half hour later Taj walks into the game room. She's dressed crazy-ass as usual, totally over the top and then some. She greets everybody in the room, but makes a point of looking around until she spots Terrence. He puts his stick down and eases over to my side. Taj comes over to us. She's all smiles and almost giddy to see him. "Hey, T, you look good, boo," she says, kissing his cheek and hugging him way too long.

"Thanks, you, too," he says, trying to keep his distance.

"I was shocked to see you standing there in the audience. I didn't know you knew my cousin."

"Your cousin?"

"Yeah, this is my aunt's house. I promised my cousin I'd hang out with him this weekend while I'm in town. Did you get to my concert last night?"

"Nah, I had to work," he says, and then he pulls me close. Taj looks at me and actually sees me standing there for the first time. I can see it in her eyes, she wants him. "I want you to meet my girl, Kenisha."

"Hey, I'm a big fan," I blatantly lie, but I guess that's what people say when they meet someone famous or kinda famous.

"Hi, you look familiar. Do I know you? Do you live in D.C.?"

"Yeah, sometimes. I go to Penn Hall."

"Oh, my God, for real, that's my old high school. I dropped out in the ninth grade. How is it, probably the same, huh?"

"Yeah, I guess," I say. Seriously, how the hell am I supposed to know if it's the same or not? For real, it sounds like girlfriend should have stayed around Penn a few more years.

She turns back to Terrence. "You know we should catch up and hang out while I'm in town. Here's my cell number. Call me."

My jaw dropped. Oh, hell, no, this bitch did not just give my lawnmower guy her cell phone number right in front of me. Terrence doesn't acknowledge it one way or the other. He takes the paper with her number on it and hands it to me. It's too obvious. She has to get that diss. "And these are our friends, Jalisa and Diamond," Terrence adds.

Jalisa and Diamond speak, but aren't as cordial as I'm trying to be. We all stand around and talk some more, then Taj moves on to another group. Terrence goes back to shooting pool, and me and my girls start talking again, this time in French. No one seems to be paying much attention to us.

Of course we're talking about what just happened. Then Jalisa reminds me that Taj was trying to get with Tyrece when he was engaged to Jade. I turn around and look at her. She's with a group on the other side of the room, but she's looking at the pool table. Correction, she's looking at Terrence standing beside the pool table. *"Putain,"* I say.

Jalisa and Diamond start laughing. Calling her a bitch in French makes it sound a lot nicer than it is. But a bitch is bitch in any language. Terrence walks over. I turn to him and smile. He slips his arms around my waist and holds me close to his body. *"Ta petite amie est une putain."*

He laughs in a way that makes me think he knows exactly what I just said to him. Then he proves it. "Bitch or not, she's not my girlfriend."

Jalisa looks at Diamond, and then they look at me. I'm still looking at Terrence. He's just smiling. "It's getting late. Are you ready to go?"

"Yeah, we're done here," I say, looking at Taj looking at me. I see the jealously in her eyes. She wants what I got, and that's just too damn bad. Terrence is *my* lawnmower guy.

Terrence says his goodbyes to his frat brothers and a few other people around. Jalisa, Diamond and I wait out on the porch as he speaks to some guys for a few minutes. When he finishes he comes over to us.

"Hey, anybody hungry?" he asks when he meets up with us.

"Yeah," we say in unison.

"All right, a couple of my friends are headed over to the fast-food place across from the mall. Do you want to go?"

"Yeah," we say in union again.

"Okay, let's do this."

We get to the car and drive off, headed to the mall. A few minutes later we pull up in the fast-food parking lot and meet up with the two guys we hung out with earlier. They were the same ones talking with Jalisa and Diamond all night. We go in, get our food, eat and just sit, talking, mostly about music and college classes.

So as we're sitting there laughing and talking another crew of friends from the party show up. They come over and sit near us and it becomes a huge party all over again. Then Taj and her entourage comes in and, of course, she comes directly to our table and sits her ass right down next to Terrence. Mostly everybody in the place is excited to see her, but I'm not and it's obvious.

"So, Kenisha, you said that you live in D.C., right?" Taj says, finally seeing that I exist.

"Sometimes," I say.

"I don't get it. What do you mean, sometimes?"

"I live with my grandmother in D.C. and on weekends I stay at my dad's house here in Virginia."

"Oh, I get it now. I sometimes do that, too. I have a place in D.C., in Atlanta, in New York and in L.A. You should come visit me in L.A," she says directly to Terrence. But he's talking to one of the guys and ignoring her. "So, Terrence, how's your mom?"

He turns to her. "She's good."

"My dad asks about the old neighborhood all the time. I think he misses it. Do you remember when he used to coach you and your brother in basketball? That was so much fun, wasn't it? We had some good times, didn't we?"

I can see Terrence flinch. He always does when someone brings up his younger brother. "Terrence, I need to get home pretty soon. Can we leave now?" I say.

"Yeah, I'm ready."

Taj looks at me like she's ready to strangle me. "We'll be here later if you still want to hang out after dropping her off."

"Nah, that's okay. I'm done for the night," he says, getting up and taking my hand. "Take care."

We say goodbye to the others, then leave. Jalisa and Diamond are smiling so hard they're about to bust. As soon as we get in the car we all start laughing. "Oh, my God, is she for real?" Jalisa says.

"I know, right, she's unbelievable," Diamond adds.

"Terrence, I know she's your girl and all, but damn, what's up?"

"I remember Taj back in the day. She always wanted to be a star. That's all she ever talked about growing up. Her mom and pops are both dead and her grandparents let her run wild. Back then she'd do anything to be the center of attention."

"But she's sixteen. She can't think that's right, can she?"

"I guess so," Jalisa says.

I just shake my head and look over to Terrence as he drives. He's looking straight ahead. I wonder what he's thinking right now and if he's wondering about being with Taj. I hope not.

It takes no time to get to the first house. Terrence drops Diamond off and then Jalisa and then he drives to my dad's house to drop me off. "Thanks, I had a great time," I say.

He nods. "I'm glad. Look, I know you're a little upset…"

"So Taj, superstar, has a crush on my lawnmower guy."

"*Had* a crush—that's all past tense, ancient history."

I shake my head. "Uh-uh, I don't think so. It definitely didn't look like past tense, ancient history to me. She wants you bad."

"Well, she can't have me bad," he jokes, then sees I am not amused. "You know she was just doing all that for the show and to get attention. She was getting everybody all hyped up, that's all. It's her job. It's all a part of what she does to entertain."

"Yeah, I know, and it worked, but still…"

He starts laughing. "Whoa, shorty is jealous," he says.

Yeah, so he's right. I am, but I'd never admit it. "I am not jealous. I'm just saying—"

"That you're jealous," he interrupts while still laughing. "Come here," he says, trying to pull me over close to him.

I refuse to go on principle.

"Come on," he says. His voice is deeper and softer. I lean in just a little closer. "Look at me," he says, turning my chin to face him. "You're my girl, okay? You're the one I want to hang with, not Taj. I don't care about all that other stuff going on with her. That's her drama, not ours. We're together. Not Taj and not Gia—you and me, okay?"

I nod my head slowly. I hear and believe him, but I also know that he and I aren't physical and that's gonna come to a head one of these days. Right now I try not to think about if or from whom he's getting it. I do know that both Gia and Taj would love to be with him. But I'm just not ready right now. I keep wondering. "What about sex," I blurt out, because I've just been thinking about it.

"What about it?"

"You're not a virgin, Terrence. I am."

"I know and I like you that way."

"You know what I mean."

He looks away and sighs heavily. I know, right then, he's about to say something I'm not gonna like. But I started it. I opened the can of worms, so I guess I need to deal with the answer, whatever it is. "Yeah, I've had sex with other girls. They offered and I did it. I'm not gonna lie to you."

I release the breath I've been holding. Okay, that wasn't as bad as I thought. Of course he realizes that I know he didn't actually admit or deny anything I didn't already know. But I accept it nonetheless. "My dad's car is here. I'd better get inside."

"Do you want me to come in, too?"

"Nah, I'm good. He's okay. Good night."

We kiss and then kiss again. I get out of the car thinking it was a good night. It doesn't matter what Taj says or does—Terrence is my lawnmower guy.

As soon as I unlock the front door and walk in I hear my name called, but this time it's not the boys. It's my dad. "Kenisha, get in here now."

"Merde." I go into my dad's office and I see him sitting behind his desk with Courtney by his side leaning on the back of his chair. She's got this plastered fake smile on her face. But I can't concentrate on her right now. My dad has this stupid frown on his face. "Do you have any idea what time it is? Where the hell were you?"

I know the question is rhetorical, but I glance at my watch anyway. Seriously, it's not that late.

"It's one-thirty in the morning. Now I don't know what your grandmother lets you get away with when you're in D.C., but all that's gonna stop right now. Do you understand? Consider yourself grounded until further notice. And that sneaking out of the house ain't gonna fly this time."

Here we go again. Seriously, does he think this is new to me? See, I hear his "you're grounded" thing all the time. If I ever paid attention to it I guess I'd be really upset, but I don't, so I'm not. I just look at him without speaking.

"Are you drunk or high or something?"

I look at him and see he's actually serious about asking me that question. Please, I can't believe he'd even say something like that to me. But I can pretty much guess where he got the idea. Courtney is standing there smiling so hard her face looks like it's about to crack. All right, she got this point, but we both know this isn't the end battle.

"That question isn't rhetorical, Kenisha. Answer me."

"Maybe she can't," Courtney whispers loud enough for me to hear her.

Okay, I gotta speak up on this madness right now. "If you knew anything about me you'd know that I don't drink alcohol and I never get high, *ever.* All that's for losers," I say, looking directly at Courtney. With that said, I go back into my silent mode. He looks at me, seeing I'm telling the truth. For real, is he kidding me with this stale bullshit about drugs and alcohol?

"You're grounded. And you have curfew. You're to be in the house no later than eight o'clock on weekdays and eleven o'clock on weekends. Understand?"

Seriously, it was all I could do not to laugh. Is he kidding? He had to be. Then it hit me; this is more of Courtney's work. I really have to come up with something very special for her.

I don't know what the hell I'm thinking staying at my dad's house after the party. Talk about drama. First of all he's not here all weekend and then when he shows up he's acting all parental. Now he starts this ridiculous lecture about how hard it is being on the streets and how worried he was all night not knowing where I was. I'm looking at him as if he's lost his mind. For real, does he really want to play the you're-not-home card?

After the brief mini-lecture, because as usual my dad quickly runs out of things to say, I turn to leave the office. Then I hear Courtney say something. "James I need a couple hundred dollars to get some things for the house tomorrow."

I turn around and see my dad go in his pocket and pull the money out. There's no argument, no conversation, not even a "For what?" He just does it. All of the sudden I get it. Courtney used me to get back in good with my dad. So as long as he's pissed at me, she'll get whatever she wants. Damn. I didn't think she was that smart. Apparently I'm wrong. Okay, as I said before, one point for her.

eleven

After the Fact

kenishi_wa K Lewis
Okay, it's time to get down to business and find out what's really going on. I need to get real. Enough of the secrets and half-truths.
29 Apr * Like * Comment * Share

Sunday morning I wake up early, but don't get out of bed right away. I just lie there staring up at the ceiling. I had another troubling dream about my mother last night. We were on the Metro train again. This time as the train was pulling off she tried to tell me something, but I couldn't hear her. I do remember that all the furniture from the storage shed was on the train with us. I keep thinking, *That's strange,* but then again, so is the dream.

So I'm lying here now trying to figure out what it means. I don't know. Then I grab my laptop to check out the prescription links Jade forwarded to me yesterday. I start searching around and wind up back at the hospital that sent the bills. She was right, there's no way to really get in and find out any information. I call Jalisa and wake her up.

"Hey, it's me. You awake?"

"No," she says groggily.

"Wake up, I have a question. It's important."

"Yeah, what's up?" she says, sounding much more awake now.

"A few weeks ago I found some hospital bills at my grand-mother's house. They were for my mom. I think my mom was sick with something when she died. I have no idea what it was. Jade doesn't know and my grandmom's not talking. Do you think since Natalie's a nurse at the hospital she could find out?"

"I don't know. I can ask her. What time is it?" she asks.

"Seven o'clock."

"Okay, she's not home right now. She's working a twelve-hour graveyard shift, so she doesn't get off until later this morning, but she should be in this afternoon. What do you think the illness was?"

"I don't know. I'm scared to even imagine. But Jade has been reading up on all those pills my mom used to take. She found out that they're serious prescribed pain pills. So why would you need all those pain pills unless you're in serous pain? And serious pain means something is seriously wrong."

"Okay, I'll ask Natalie as soon as she gets home. Do you want to catch up later on today?"

"Yeah, why don't we meet up at the mall? Jade's supposed to pick me up, so I'll have her get me there."

"Okay, I'll tell Diamond, too. I'll text you with a time to meet."

"Okay, thanks, Jalisa, and thank Natalie for me. Bye."

As soon as I hang up I go right back to trying to figure out my mom's bills. I spend the next two hours and still I hit a brick wall. I decide to hold up and check out the other thing I need to figure out.

When my mom and I first got kicked out of the house I accidentally brought my dad's personal laptop with me. I gave it back, of course, but after I copied all of his files first. Now granted, most of these files are about the business and pretty much out of date by now, but I remember there were a few personal files, as well.

I go in and start pulling them up. Luckily with each upgrade laptop my dad gives me, I upload all of my previous files including his. So I go through what I have and I see that it's not really much. At least nothing I can figure out. So since there's nobody home, I decide to upgrade my "daddy" files. Unlike Courtney's brother, Cash, who I caught going through my dad's computer a few weeks ago, I know exactly what I'm doing. I grab my 8 GB flash drive and head to my dad's downstairs office.

It takes a little longer to get in than I thought it would. My dad changed his password, but he's pretty predictable. So, I figure it out and I'm in and finally copy all his folders and files onto my flash drive. Then I hear the front door close. "Shit." Somebody's coming. I figure I can hide, abort or keep going. Then I hear Courtney on her cell phone bitching about my dad and money. I decide to keep going. Her voice is getting louder, so I know she's coming this way. I kick my feet up on the desk, shrink what I'm doing and pull up a video site on the screen just as she ends her phone call and walks in.

"Hey, what are you doing in here?" she asks, obviously surprised to see me sitting at my dad's desk.

I look up, seeing her standing in the office doorway, then go back to copying files and watching a Taj video.

"I asked you a question, Kenisha," she says, coming into

the office. "What are you doing in here. Why are you using your father's computer? How did you even get on it?"

I still don't respond. I just keep doing what I'm doing, copying files. "You know I'm gonna tell him," she says, smiling happily, thinking she has something else on me. But I still don't respond.

"Kenisha, Kenisha," she says, coming closer.

Just then I finish copying the last file. I grab the flash drive and start closing screens and backing out of the computer. So right now there's no way anyone can tell I was even there. I even grab a tissue and wipe the top off.

"What are you doing on his computer?" Courtney asks, walking over to the desk and opening the laptop I just closed. She tries to check out what I was doing, but sees it's back to being password protected. "Can you open his files again?"

I still don't say anything. I just get up and walk out of the office. I go back upstairs to my bedroom and sit at my desk and open a book. I close my door, uselessly knowing, of course, that Courtney will be coming in soon. I'm right. She's here. She just barges in. "Kenisha, do you know your father's password?"

I look up from my book and do the fake smile like she did last night. "Oh, hi, Courtney, I didn't hear you come in. Good morning. Where is everybody?"

"What the hell are you talking about? You didn't see me come in? You were just in your dad's office. You looked right at me. You saw me."

I give her a blank expression, then frown and shake my head. "I don't know what you're talking about."

She glares at me all evil-looking as usual. "You know

damn well what I'm talking about. I just saw you down-stairs in your father's office on his computer."

"I'm reading my book," I say.

"Don't lie to me, Kenisha. I just saw you."

Of course I'm looking at her like she's crazy and the fact that she's all upset and about to start screaming doesn't help her case. "I just saw you downstairs. You know I'm gonna tell your father."

"Tell him what?" I ask innocently. "That I'm upstairs in my bedroom reading my book?"

"No, that you were on his computer."

"It's password protected. How can I possible get on his computer?" I ask innocently.

"You know his password, don't you? What is it?"

I lean back in my chair and look up at her, shaking my head. "You know you used to be a lot calmer when your brother, Cash, was hanging around the house. It's a shame he's doing active duty in the Marines again. He was the only one in this house that had some sense, except for Jr. and Jason, of course."

"Your lame insults don't move me, Kenisha. What's your father's password? Tell me or I'll tell him what you were doing."

"Fine, then I'll post the video of you and your attorney trying to scam my dad on the internet."

"No, you won't," she says only half-assured.

I give her another blank stare. Is she kidding? Why the hell would I tell her? So the blank stare continues for about a minute and a half. She finally guesses that I'm not telling her shit.

"You are such a bitch," she hisses, then turns around, storms out and slams my bedroom door behind her.

Okay, I just can't let her get away with that. I get up quickly and open the door. "Courtney," I call out. She's halfway down the hall, but turns. "Do you know anything about my dad's other family in Maryland?"

Her eyes get big and her jaw drops. "His what?"

I shake my head. She doesn't know. "Never mind," I say sweetly, and close my bedroom door again.

I sit back down and smile—one point for me. I open my laptop and insert the flash drive, then start going through all the file documents I just copied. A lot of files mention Maryland addresses, so I start checking them out. I come up blank.

Then I look at my dad's bank records. Seriously, he really needs to stop using the same password for everything. There are the typical monthly checks and I can figure most of them out. But one seems odd and I can't find anything else about it at all. It's pay to the order of Reba Clark and there's an address. I look the name up on the computer and then in the yellow pages. Nothing. So I go to Google maps, then enter the address and see the location at ground level. It shows an intersection. But the closest I can get is about three blocks away. But it does look like a residential area, so I start to wonder who lives at that address.

My cell phone beeps. I have a text message. Thinking its Jalisa, I still check the caller ID. It's Jade. Hey, I text.

You're up? she texts, obviously surprised.

Yeah, I've been on the computer trying to figure Mom's hospital bills out. I can't find anything. Did you find anything else?

No.

I asked Jalisa to ask Natalie to help us out. I don't know if she can do anything. I hope so. I'm meeting Jalisa at the mall. Can you pick me up there?

Yeah, what time?

I don't know yet. I'll text you. So what happened to you last night?

What do you mean?

The frat party, I thought you were going.

Long story, we'll talk about that later, she says cryptically. I gotta go, text me with a time.

Okay, later.

So now I text my grandmother to check in to see what's up with her. She's not exactly good at texting, but she's getting better. Before, it used to take her twenty minutes to reply with tons of typos, now it takes her about ten minutes to reply. It's good to see she's still trying. When I get her message back I smile. She's doing fine and glad she went to visit her sister.

I grab a quick shower, throw on some clothes and chill out the rest of the morning, then I meet Jalisa and Diamond at the mall. We basically talk about school stuff. We don't really feel like shopping, but still we get a few things. I find something that's perfect for Jade, so I pick it up. I do that a lot now. She's always getting stuff for me and now I get stuff for her, too. Sisters, right. Afterward we just hang in the food court checking out the sights.

twelve

Mirror, Mirror on the Wall—WTF

kenishi_wa K Lewis
When you don't see craziness coming, you don't get a chance to get out of the way. So is this craziness?
29 Apr * Like * Comment * Share

"Seriously, y'all, compared to the guys at the party last night, these high school boys are pathetic. Look at them running around throwing food at one another like its kindergarten recess," Diamond says, shaking her head.

"You know what they say, boys will be boys." Jalisa sighs while yawning.

"So when do they grow up?" Diamond adds.

"Never," I say.

"Yeah, I guess you're right about that."

"My dad grounded me with a curfew last night," I say.

"He did? Why? You didn't get in that late."

"I think Courtney got him to do it. She figured out the enemy of my enemy is my friend. If she keeps my dad pissed at me, she can get whatever she wants from him. Its psychology 101 and he's falling for it."

"Like you say, they never grow up."

"What are you gonna do?"

"I'll figure something out."

"Wait, oh, my God, I can't believe we've been together all afternoon and didn't talk about Taj. Can you believe her last night?" Diamond says excitedly, totally changing the subject. She's right, nobody brought her up earlier. We just start laughing.

"I looked her up on Wikipedia when I got home last night," Jalisa says. "For real, I can't believe she's our age."

"She dropped out of high school in ninth grade," I say.

"That is so stupid," Diamond says.

"I know, right," Jalisa adds, "and she looks so old with all that makeup. And what the hell was she wearing even after the miniconcert when she was in the game room?"

"A black fishnet bodysuit with a fluorescent thong and pasties covering only her nipples," Diamond says, shaking her head. "She really needs a stylist…"

"And how about a couple of Prozac to calm her ass down. Did you see how she was on Terrence last night?"

"Damn, I know. But I like how he kept shutting her down." Diamond laughs. "What did you do with her phone number?"

I shake my head. "I forgot all about it. I think I just stuffed it in my pocket. It's probably still there."

"Crank calls!" both Jalisa and Diamond say together. We start laughing all over again.

"No, but seriously, she is on Terrence hard. She's so obvious. I can't believe the skank just, like, gave him her cell number right in front of me after he introduced me as his girl."

"You're right, she's a skank," Diamond adds.

"And she's a cheap knockoff of about twenty other shock

stars. She can't even sing. I heard all her concerts are lip-sync."

"And, oh, my God, she can't even dance." We laugh again.

"I know, right. Did you see her trying to keep up with us?"

"She was pathetic and everybody was seeing that."

"Yep, that's why she stopped and pulled on Terrence."

"All she does is that grinding pole-dancing shit."

"For real," I say as my cell rings. I check caller ID, then answer. "Hey, Jade."

"Hey, I'm outside the mall. Are you ready?"

"Yeah, I'll be right out. What entrance?"

"I'm almost at the food court," she says.

"Okay, I'll be right outside. See ya." I close my cell and look at my girls. While I was talking to Jade they were still making fun of Taj. "Jade's outside, I gotta go." I stand up and grab my stuff. Jalisa and Diamond do the same.

"Yeah, we gotta go, too. I still have SAT studying to do."

"Me, too," Jalisa says.

"Yeah, me, too," I say.

We walk outside and I see Jade's car stopped at the traffic light across the street. "A'ight, I gotta go. I'll see you guys later." We hug, say goodbye again just as Jade pulls up. They say hi and bye and I climb into the car and wave to them.

"Did you eat?" Jade asks me as soon as she pulls off.

"No, not yet, did you?"

"No. Let's grab some takeout in D.C., then go home. I have an exam to study for and about ten chapters to read."

"Sounds good, I need to study for my SATs."

We talk about me taking the SATs and what to study as we wait in the take-out line. We order cheese steaks and fries, get our food and then go home. We turn off and reset the alarm system and then head straight to the kitchen and start eating. "Mmm, this smells so good."

"I know it does, and I'm starved."

"Me, too," I say, and then we dig in. After about three bites of my sandwich and a dozen French fries, I take a sip of my orange soda and start laughing. Jade looks over at me like I just lost my mind and I start smiling. "I forgot to tell you, I got a text message from Grandmom this morning. She's doing good," I say.

"Good," she says, then chuckles, shaking her head. "You know, I still can't believe you're getting her technology-savvy. Every time I get a text message from her it cracks me up."

"I told her she had to come into the twenty-first century. She just laughs, saying she has no choice with me living in the house. But I'm just glad she's actually doing it, and you know what? She's getting pretty good, too."

"I know, right. Who'd have thought?"

We laugh. Then a few moments of silence pass between us as I take another bite and chew slowly. "Um," I begin slowly, "Jalisa talked to Natalie about looking into Mom's hospital records. She said she can't get into the records room."

"I didn't think so," Jade says.

I just nod silently. "I gotta tell you something," I say.

"What?" she asks, looking at me.

"I've been having all these strange dreams about Mom lately. I don't know why—they come almost every night."

"Kenisha, you gotta let it go."

"I know."

"What kind of dreams are they?"

"They're not scary or anything. In most of them I'm on

the Metro with Mom. She's telling me that she's okay and everything's fine. But she's not really talking, but I understand what she means. I also tell her what's been going on with me and you and everybody. Then the train stops at this station. I get off and Mom stays on. She just smiles and waves goodbye. In last night's dream I saw all the furniture from storage on the train with her like she was taking it someplace."

"That's funny. I was just thinking about the furniture the other day. What would you think if we sold some of it to raise money to help pay off some of the hospital bill?"

"Uh-uh, no way, that's Mom's furniture. It's all we have left of her. No."

"Kenisha, think. We need the money to pay the hospital bill. Grandmom doesn't have it and I'm not gonna have her risk this house. We have to do something. This is it."

I stop eating and think a moment. At first I'm still a little upset. Then I start thinking about it and also about my dream. Maybe my mom is telling me it's time to let go of things. I never really considered what to do with the furniture before. After we cleared out the house it was always just there in the background of drama. Right now it's in a huge storage bin that costs a fortune each month. Jade's right, we could definitely use the money now. "Okay, but maybe we can keep a few pieces for ourselves."

"Sure, of course," Jade says.

"You know, Mom had really good taste and the antique furniture is probably worth a lot of money. It's a good idea to sell some of it. Plus, we won't have that huge storage bill. We can store whatever we want to keep in something smaller."

"I'll call around and check out some consignment shops tomorrow and see what they say."

"Is selling the furniture gonna be enough?"

Jade shakes her head. "No, probably not. We're gonna need a lot more money and we just don't have it. Our college fund is legally untouchable and the trust funds Mom left us won't mature until we're either twenty-five or graduate from college."

"I don't think the hospital will wait that long to get paid. They've already sent a couple of past-due invoices. We need big money now," I say.

"Don't worry, we'll figure something out."

"How can I not worry about it? What if they come after Grandmom and try to take the house? You know how much she loves this place. It would kill her. We can't let that happen."

"It won't come to that, trust me."

"Are you gonna ask Tyrece for the money?"

"No."

"Then what?"

Jade doesn't answer, so I don't push it. I know she's as upset as I am. I also know that neither one of us can really do anything right now.

"Something will come up. It always does."

"Yeah, okay," I halfheartedly agree, then start eating again. I don't buy the whole wishful thinking. I gotta do something. I can't just wait and hope.

"So, tell me about the party last night. How was it?"

"It was nice, then it got crazy. Why didn't you come?"

She shook her head. "Taj and I don't exactly do well in the same room."

"I can definitely see that. For real, she is sick. She went all buck wild last night—talk about a hot mess."

"She has serious impulse-control issues and she refuses to leave her character onstage."

"What do you mean?" I ask.

"If you're gonna take on a persona for fans, you need to keep something real in your life, something or someone normal that's not affected by all the hype. That person grounds you. Then you can leave that 'star' character onstage and be yourself. She's confused because she's 'that' character all the time."

I get what she's saying. "Is that what happened before with you and Tyrece—he started believing the hype?"

"Yeah, and I wasn't about to go there with him."

"You're his normal."

She nods. "Yeah, something like that."

"Are you two gonna get back together?"

"Check you out," she says, smiling, "all up in my personal business."

"Yeah, so, we're sisters. I'm supposed to be. So tell me. What's the deal? Are y'all getting back together?"

"He wants to, and I'm thinking about it. He still loves me."

"Do you love him?"

She nods slowly. "But there's a lot more to it."

"Taj."

"Yes, plus other things. I need to trust him. I'm not sure we're at that point anymore. Before I could listen to all the crap out there and it wouldn't phase me. But now, I don't know."

"I like Tyrece. I hope you guys get back together."

She shrugs. I shake my head. "You know, I couldn't believe Taj. She was all up in Terrence's face. She even gave him her cell phone number right in front of me."

Jade shakes her head, then glances over at me. "What did he do with it?"

I start laughing. "He gave it to me right in front of her. I don't think she was happy." We start laughing again.

"I always liked T," Jade says.

My cell phone beeps. I check my caller ID. Since I don't recognize the number or the area code, I just close my phone and don't answer. So we start talking about Taj and all the drama Jade put up with when she was engaged to Tyrece and when he was producing Taj's CD. "Do you think there was ever really anything between Taj and Tyrece?"

Jade takes a deep breath and exhales slowly. "I know there was. But if you're asking whether or not they had sex, he says they didn't, but I don't know. His career and his life are two different things, I know that, but sometimes it's hard."

"I can't believe Taj—she's my age and she acts like a total slut onstage and off."

"She thinks that's gonna make her famous, but it's not—it makes her stupid," Jade says.

I nod, agreeing, and think about my frenemy, Chili. It was the same thing. We were friends once. Now she sleeps with anybody to get what she wants. She even slept with my ex-boyfriend, LaVon, thinking he was gonna marry her and she'd be a NBA basketball wife. She was wrong. "Mom always said that your reputation is the one thing you can never lose."

"I know. She was right."

We finish eating and start cleaning up the kitchen. Afterward we get the trash together and take it to the curb. Then we sit outside a minute, laughing and talking about the people in the neighborhood and things we remember growing up. When we go back inside I hear my cell phone beeping. I have messages. I have a text from Terrence and Jalisa and a voice message from the same phone number I didn't recognize before. I listen.

"Kenisha, this is Taj from the party last night. Listen, I just saw your dance video on Facebook. You're good, not professional or anything like that, but you have something going on. So, I was wondering if you'd be interested in doing something with me in my upcoming video. It's gonna be released as an internet download only. Rehearsals start Monday at five and we shoot video in a couple of weeks right here in the city. There's seriously good money to be made. Oh, and the offer goes to your girlfriends, too. Y'all have to audition first, though. Let me know if you're interested as soon as you can. Hit me up, we'll talk."

"Oh. My. God!" I say excitedly.

"What?" Jade says, looking at me.

I start laughing giddily. "Oh, my God, for real, you are never gonna believe who just left me a voice message."

"Who?"

"Taj!"

"What?"

"Taj—listen, listen," I say, replaying the message for her. She takes my cell phone and listens to the message. Her expression changes instantly. My excitement over Taj's voice message is seriously short-lived as soon as Jade hears the message. The first thing she says is, "Oh, hell, no," then she really starts going off.

"What do you mean?"

"Taj is a user, Kenisha. Don't trust her. No."

"Did you not hear the part about seriously good money to be made?"

"For her, yeah, that's what she does. She uses people to get what she wants and to benefit her. She's not looking to help you or anyone else."

"Jade, look, I know she's got serious skank issues and she went after Ty and Terrence, but if I can get some money from her just by dancing I don't see why not do it."

"Because it's never that simple with Taj. You think you know her, but you don't."

I didn't respond or say anything more. I know Jade isn't going to change her mind about this. She has the same look in her eye that Mom did when I told her I wanted to get my belly button pierced and a tattoo. Talking to her about it isn't gonna get me anywhere so I drop it.

As soon as I get upstairs I video-call Jalisa and Diamond. I'm gonna do this and I want them with me. Their images come up instantly. "Hey, ladies, I've got some crazy insane news."

"What?" Jalisa and Diamond say.

"Taj called me and left a message."

"Taj," Diamond says.

"Yeah, wait, there's more."

"What the hell does she want calling you?" Jalisa adds.

"She really likes our dancing and she's got a dance job for us. She wants us in her next video. Rehearsals are Monday at five o'clock. Are you up for it?"

Jalisa's jaw drops and Diamond starts laughing. See, this is why I like doing video calls. I get to see their reactions instantly. They're totally shocked.

"Seriously," Jalisa finally says, "is she for real, no way."

"Yeah, she's very serious," I say.

Diamond laughs again. "Oh, my God, I can't believe her. She actually asked you something like that. What a skank.

Does she really expect us to do this after all the shit she did to you at the party?"

"What do you mean?" I ask seriously with no clue here.

"What, are you kidding me? She treated you like you were nothing. If you had turned your back for half a second she would have been all up on top of Terrence in a hot minute," Jalisa says.

"I'm serious, she is such a bitch," Diamond says.

So right now they're seriously going off on Taj and I'm seriously not getting it. Yes, she's a bitch, and yes, she's a skank, but she's also someone who can get us paid to dance. "Okay, but what about the money she's offering?"

"Girl, you know video dancers don't get paid much money."

"Sure they do. They're dancers."

"No way they get paid."

"Here, I just looked it up. It says that nonunion music video dancers get about four hundred and seventy-five dollars a day. Overtime is like sixty-five dollars an hour and rehearsals are about two hundred and fifty dollars."

"So if rehearsals for the video are tomorrow we can make, like, two hundred fifty dollars each, right. That's standard rates," I say.

"Please, do you really think Taj is gonna pay us that?"

"Sure, why not?"

"I don't trust her, so I'm not doing it," Jalisa says.

"For real, you can count me out, too," Diamond adds.

"So that's the three of us telling her to go to hell," Jalisa says, assuming I say no, as well.

But I don't say anything and they don't notice because we immediately go on to another topic of conversation. We start talking about taking the SATs and studying together.

Then that segues to our usual picking-colleges conversations and then finally to guys and dating. We laugh and talk for the next hour. But still in the back of my mind I'm thinking about dancing in the video. What's a few hours dancing to get paid? I don't like her, but I'll definitely take her money.

What really bothers me is everybody around me. They all think they know what's best for me, but they don't. I can do this. I can get the money and get the hospital off Grandmom's back. As soon as we disconnect I call Taj. She's not there so I leave a message telling her that I'm in. I just won't tell anybody, not even my girls.

thirteen

Got Haters?

kenishi_wa K Lewis
Hating on others only makes you look desperate and stupid and shows everybody how insecure you really are. Get over yourself. Stop hating!
30 Apr * Like * Comment * Share

seriously, it's never a dull day here at the Penn. It's Monday morning, I'm back at school and, wouldn't you know it, drama hits as soon as I walk in the building. The halls are already lined with the usual respective groups. The jocks hang in the hall by the gym. The cheerleaders hover just a few feet away. Then there's the geeks, the Latinos, the Africans, the Middle Easterners, the rappers, the rockers, the brains—everybody has their hallway place except me. I don't really fit into any of the groups, so I just have me.

At one point the popular kids tried to hook me, but that wasn't gonna happen. So the thing is they're all kinda looking at me now, more than usual. I have no idea why and right now I really don't care. I would think it's all just my imagination, but my life doesn't work like that.

Anyway, I haul myself in extra early so I can get to class without seeing anybody. Apparently that's not gonna happen. Forget this—I walk to my locker and, as usual, try to get the day over as quickly as possible.

"Kenisha, Kenisha, hey, there you are. I've been looking everywhere for you." Neeka rushes up to me, hooks her arm in mine and steers me toward my locker and then starts whispering. "All right, girl, tell me everything."

"What do you mean, tell you what?"

"Okay, first you have this kick-ass YouTube video with you dancing and now you have all these—"

"Wait, wait, that video was supposed to be taken down over the weekend," I correct.

"I don't know if it's down or not. You know how it is, people be moving stuff around on the internet all the time. I know you're on Twitter and Facebook, so you're probably on everything else, too. You know nothing ever disappears once it's out there and it looks like your dance video is seriously out there and about to go viral. I never knew anyone go viral before," she says, then she looks at me like I just split an atom with my mind.

After that I didn't want to hear any more. I knew Neeka was probably right. File sharing on the internet is like having a hot secret—nobody keeps it to themselves—and apparently I'm the latest hot secret to go around. "Okay, this is just too stupid," I say, shaking my head. I start spinning the lock on my locker, but don't get a chance to set the first number.

"Wait, so now there are all these pictures posted of you hanging out and dancing with Taj. I am too impressed. But, girl, why the hell didn't you tell me you were in like that and hanging with her this weekend? Shit, why didn't you take me with you?"

"Pictures posted," I repeat, 'cause that was really all I was hearing. She starts explaining what she saw posted. See, this is why I hate cell phone cameras and irresponsible idiots. They take pictures and post them to make people think they're popular when they're really not. "I wasn't hangin' with Taj, she was hangin' with me," I say, then start spinning my combination, but then she stops me again.

"Wait, wait, there's more. We were talking before and you're never gonna guess who transferred here from Hazelhurst."

I don't get the chance to guess 'cause I see exactly who it is as soon as I turn around to look at her. Regan Payne walks down the hall. She sees me and I see her. I swear my jaw just drops. Of all the people, why the hell does it have to be her?

"Hey, Neeka," Regan says as she passes us, then eyes me hard like she's got something to say to me.

I eye her, too. See, we've played this game before and I will definitely step up to her again. Seriously, if she thinks I won't do a repeat on kicking her ass here at Penn, she's delusional. I will and I'll enjoy it. I'm still not over her calling my mom out like she did. As a matter of fact, she's lucky I don't start something up right now. They'll be calling her "hallway hair" in both schools.

"Hey."

I turn around. Troy is standing right behind me. He's smiling. I still haven't figured out his game. "Hey," I say.

Neeka looks at both of us. "Neeka, this is Troy." She smiles and nods and does that thing most girls do when they see him—mouth open, eyes glazed, stupid smile on face.

"Hey," he says, then nods his head.

"Hey," Neeka says, then looks at me, "we'll talk later."

As soon as she walks away Troy steps into her space and

blocks my view of Regan. "I tried to call you Sunday to see if you wanted to hang out," he says.

I just look at him. He's been asking this same question since the day I walked into the Penn. He knows it's not gonna happen. "Funny, I thought we got past this point. I guess not."

"That's not what I mean. I was thinking we can really hang. You know, go to a movie or something."

"I usually hang with Terrence, my boyfriend."

"Look, it doesn't have to be a thing, it's just hanging."

I look at him. He looks sincere, but I've been fooled before. "I'll think about it," I say, and then let my eyes drift to the side where Regan is standing staring at us.

Troy glances to the side, too. Regan quickly looks away, pretending she wasn't just eyeing me. *Okay,* I'm thinking, *what's all that about?*

"I guess you see my cousin transferred here," he says.

Shit, I completely forgot he told me before that Regan is his cousin. I glance around him again. Regan is back to staring at me. "Yeah, I noticed."

"I didn't know she was coming until it was already set."

"No big deal. She's your cousin. She just needs to stay out of my face. She can stay on her side and I'll stay on mine."

"Just like that, huh."

"Yeah, just like that. But if she wants to start something, I'm not gonna back down or walk away."

"I talked to her. She's cool."

"You talked to her and she's cool. Yeah, right," I say skeptically. "Forgive me if I don't buy that. Somehow I doubt she's gonna be acting brand-new."

"She listens to me. She doesn't have a choice."

"What does that mean?" I ask him, 'cause I have no idea.

"Let's just say she listens to me," he repeats.

I still have no idea what he's talking about, but I guess it's a family thing. So whatever, either way I'm ready for whatever comes.

"You don't trust easily, do you?" he asks while pulling books out of his locker.

I start laughing. I figure he must be joking. Trusting him is like trusting Darien—it's never gonna happen. The first bell rings. "All right, whatever, I gotta get to class. Just take care of your cousin and we won't have a problem."

I get the rest of my books out of my locker. When I close it I turn around and see Neeka smiling all up in Regan's face. Okay, this is all of the sudden looking too shady. First she's with me and now she's with Regan. But I'm not saying that my friends can't be friends with other people—I'm just surprised. I got the impression she didn't like her, either. Guess I was wrong. Regan says something to Neeka and they both turn around to look at me. Regan glares, like she usually does, and Neeka just looks caught.

Enough of this. I grab my books, slam my locker closed and head to my first period. I'm the first person in class, right. That's good. I don't feel like a whole lot of staring. I get to my seat and open my cell phone to check messages. It's nothing really interesting, so I send a quick text to both Jalisa and Diamond about the internet pictures just in case they haven't heard yet.

"Hey, girl."

I look up, seeing Ursula walking over to me. Her assigned seat is across the room, but she comes in and sits in the seat right next to me. "Hey, what's going on?" I say.

"You, apparently. It's all over school about you hanging

with Taj over the weekend. Okay, question—did y'all really drive up to New York to hang with Jay-Z and Beyoncé?"

"What? No, of course not," I say.

Ursula laughs. "I didn't think so. People be lying their asses off around here. But seriously, girl, you got just about everybody talking about you right now."

"I don't know why. It was no big deal. We were just at the same party and I was dancing with my girls. You know how we do. Somebody took pictures and posted them."

"Taj," she says, shaking her head. "I remember her crazy ass when she used to hang around the way. She had this thing for Darien for a while. She loves herself some bad boys. And for real, she'd give it up in a hot minute. Most of the guys around know that for a fact."

I start chuckling—Taj and Darien together. Why am I not surprised by that? Darien is as bad as they get. He's perfect for her. The attendance bell rings and the rest of the class come in and start taking their seats. "We'll talk at lunch," she whispers as our teacher walks in and starts talking.

She gets up and goes back across the room to her assigned seat. A few minutes later class starts with a pop quiz. I'm not really prepared, but the quiz seems easy enough. I finish it and then just chill. All I'm thinking about right now is hooking up with Taj and getting paid.

After class some of the students sitting around me start asking me about Taj, but I just blow them off with bullshit answers. I don't really want to be bothered. It happens the same way in each of my classes after that. I decide to skip the cafeteria at lunch and instead hang out in the library with the computer geeks. I know it's usually pretty quiet and nobody's gonna bug me. I go in and take a seat in the back in the stacks. I put my earbuds in and put my head down. Just as I'm about to close my eyes and take a serious timeout I hear a lot of laughing and talking. Then somebody touches my shoulder. "Hey, didn't I tell you, we're famous."

"Shit," I mutter as I look up seeing Li'l T popping his ass down in the seat across from me. "Want do you want?"

"Hey, hey, hey, I know you feeling me now," Li'l T says.

"I don't even want to talk to you."

"Hey, what, I took the video down."

"Yeah, but it's too late. It's already out there. Do you know how much drama I have to deal with because of your little production?"

"Yo, that wasn't me. I wasn't the one hanging with Taj all weekend and taking pictures. So, speaking of hanging with Taj, when you gonna hook a brotha up? I need to get in there."

I start laughing, 'cause for real his mom must have dropped him on his head from a sixth-floor window. He's totally clueless.

"I gotta get out of here," I say, then start gathering my stuff just as my cell phone rings. I check caller ID, then answer. "Hey."

"Kenisha, this is Taj. Are you in?"

"Yeah, I'm in."

"Good, what about your girls?"

"They're already tied up, so they have to pass."

"A'ight, that's cool. I'm texting you the address to rehearsals today. It starts at five o'clock in Studio A, top floor. Don't be late. My time is valuable."

"Okay, see you then. Bye." I close my cell and start smiling. This is exactly what I need. I text Jalisa and Diamond

and tell them we need to talk. Then I leave a simple message—Taj wants us in her next video, are you in?

"Who was that?" Li'l T says.

I completely forgot about him. "See ya."

"Hey, wait."

I just keep going. I can't believe it—Li'l T was right. The
YouTube video is opening all kinds of doors. Now hopefully it's gonna make me some serious money, too.

So now just about everybody's talking about my song and
my dancing. By the end of the day it's all over the school.
People who I don't even know are coming up to me talking
about it and asking me questions. Then, of course, there's
the flip side of all that with the haters. You know they're
out in full force.

But seriously, thank God it's turning out to be one of
those quick days that when you blink it goes by in a flash,
'cause I don't know if I could take any more. I have people
coming up to me all day long talking about the video and
the pictures of me and about dancing with Taj. By the end
of the day I'm through. It was nonstop stupidity.

So I'm standing at my locker getting my jacket and stuff
and the drama continues. It's not like I don't hear her. She
makes damn sure I do. Seriously, jealously is a bitch named
Cassie. Every time I see her I get pissed off. She screwed
me and she acts like she's the victim.

Bottom line, Cassie is such a hater and now she's hanging with these juvenile delinquent ninth graders that don't
know any better than to take everything she says as truth.
I have a feeling she was the one who broke into my house
with Darien. I just wish I could prove it, so I can see her
ass locked up for a while.

"...yeah, I saw her on YouTube acting like she all that.

Don't nobody care about her stuck-up ass," Cassie says just loud enough so I can hear her as she walks by. I know she's talking about me, but I just shake my head. It's all stupid drama that I don't need to be bothered with right now. I have a dance audition in four hours. So, F this.

Fourteen

Going Viral in the Real World

kenishi_wa K Lewis
I never ask to be popular. It always kinda just happens. I do my thing and the world tunes in. I'm okay with it sometimes, but other times it's all just BS. Cue spotlight.
30 Apr * Like * Comment * Share

AFTER a beginning of the line to the end of the line Metro ride, I get to Maryland a few minutes earlier than I expect. The rehearsal studio is right across from the station. I walk in and look around, then head to the second floor. The studio is huge and looks nothing like the ones at Freeman studio. These are way better.

Full-length wall-to-wall mirrors surround the room on all sides. There's a piano and drum set in the corner, sprung wood floors with Marley coverings and a serious sound system. There are four other dancers sitting around laughing and talking. They look at me as soon as I walk in. I go over to them. "Hi," I say, walking up to one of the girls closest to the door. "Is this Studio A?"

"Yes, but this is a private rehearsal."

I nod. "Is this where Taj rehearses?"

"Yeah," she says, "but she's not here and she doesn't do the autograph or groupie thing when she's rehearsing. So you're gonna have to leave."

"Oh, no, I'm Kenisha Lewis. I'm supposed to be auditioning here today."

The other girls sitting around suddenly get interested in what I just said. They look over at me and then eye me up and down. I know it doesn't mean anything, so I just ignore them. "You're the new girl."

"Yeah, I guess so."

"I'm Pamela. This is Donna, Connie and my cousin Linda."

I smile at the dancers, knowing there's no way I'm gonna remember their names right now. I'm too nervous. "Hey," I say. They all speak and seem nice enough.

"So what do I do, start stretching or something?"

"Nah, first you gotta go to the office over there and speak with the manager and choreographer. They'll probably have papers for you to sign."

"What kind of papers?"

"You know, the usual legal stuff, standard release papers."

I guess I still look puzzled, because she gives me this really strained look like I'm about to walk into the middle of something crazy totally unprepared. But right now I really don't care. All I'm thinking about is stepping up my game and making some money to help my grandmother. So I go into the office and introduce myself to the two men there. The manager, Devon, starts asking me all these questions, then the choreographer, Magic Man, interrupts. "Can't you do that later? I have to get rehearsals started now. Taj is on her way. We're renting this place by the hour and I need all the time I can get."

Devon looks at his watch and nods. "All right, we'll do this afterward. Here, just sign these," he says, picking up a large white envelope from the desk and handing it to me.

"What are they?" I ask, taking the envelope from him. I open it up and pull out about twenty pages. It's all tiny type that I can barely read, so I have no idea what it says.

"They're standard release forms. They primarily state that what you do in here is the sole intellectual property of Taj Enterprises and can't be duplicated outside this studio."

"What does that mean?"

"You can't do any of my routines outside of these walls," Magic Man says. "Now, tell me about your dancing."

I give him the basic rundown on my skills. He doesn't seem to be at all impressed.

"So, you've never danced professionally," he concludes. I shake my head. "Good Lord, I don't know where Taj gets these people. Everybody wants to be a dancer but, honey, not everybody can." He grabs his water bottle and a CD from the desk.

"I understand," I say quietly. I'm just about to tell him that I'm really good, but I decide to instead show him.

"Okay," he says, already apparently exasperated, then rolls his eyes. I know he's already made up his mind about me. But I need to prove him wrong. "You're gonna have to audition. Have you ever danced with a professional dancer at least?"

"Yes, I've danced with Gayle Harmon."

His eyes light up. He looks impressed. "Really," he says.

"Yes, she's a friend of the family."

"Okay, let's see what you've got. Come on." Magic Man opens the office door and I follow.

"Wait, we're not through here yet. She has to sign these

papers before she starts." Devon hands me a pen and points to where I'm supposed to initial and sign.

"I need to read these, don't I?"

"No, just sign," Devon says.

"Come on, she can read them on break and sign after we finish practice. If she's no good, signing a bunch of papers won't matter, anyway. She'll be out of here in five minutes."

Devon takes a deep breath, then exhales quickly. "Okay, fine. Go. If you get this I want those papers signed today."

I nod, then stuff the white envelope in the bottom of my dance bag, then look at Magic Man.

"Come on, let's do this," he says hurriedly. When we get out into the studio he asks me to change, stretch, 'cause he wants to see what I can do. I agree and do as he asks. About fifteen minutes later I step into the center of the room. The other dancers are sitting around watching me. So the music comes on. It's one of Taj's songs. It's hard and loud with a fast upbeat tempo. Magic Man tells me to just do some free-style dance. I do. After a while I can tell they're impressed.

The other dancers start nodding their heads and applauding at some of my steps. Magic Man brings them up to the floor and does a dance step for us to follow. We all get it instantly. Then he adds on more steps to make it a routine. We're dancing and he's telling us to do something different or turn a different direction. It's working out great.

So, an hour and a half goes by and we're still dancing. Finally Taj shows up with her entourage of two girls and two guys. She's dressed in her usual crazy-ass style with six-inch stilettos. She doesn't speak to me or the dancers and it seems they really don't care. There's a conversation with her manager, which quickly turns into an almost-argument. Then Magic Man puts her in front of us and the music plays. We all start doing the routine he just taught us. We hold the line and it looks great, but it's obvious he's not happy. He has this perpetual frown on his face. Then it's all of a sudden plain to see that Taj can't dance. All she can do is shake her weave around and wiggle her ass.

We do the same routine over and over again and she's still not getting it. At one point we're getting back to the opening position and I just can't take it anymore. "Damn, is she really this bad?" I mutter.

"She's gonna be even worse when we get to the video set."

"What do you mean?"

Linda and Pam chuckle. "You'll see."

We do the routine a few more times. She still misses the mark. But it's not like it's at the same place. She misses it everywhere. After the seventh time Magic Man completely changes her part of the routine. Now it looks more like a pole dance minus the pole. She grinds, she gyrates and she aces it. She's finally happy. Then the door opens and an older woman with green streaks in her hair walks in carrying some bags. She motions toward us. Linda walks over and takes one of the shopping bags. She opens it and starts handing out smaller bags.

"What's this?" I ask, hoping its swag of something good.

"It's our costume for the video."

I look at the size of the bag. They've got to be kidding. It's like an elementary school lunch bag. I open mine. There's a thonglike mini and what looks like two circle Band-Aids on some string. "Are they serious?" I ask. "Where's the rest of it?"

"We'll get the stiletto boots at the shoot."

"Seriously, this is all we're supposed to wear?"

Nobody answers, then a few seconds later the door opens and this guy walks in. He's dressed in a perfectly fitted business suit and expensive shoes. He looks around, sees Taj and then keeps looking around. Taj stops dancing instantly and runs over to him excitedly. "Eric, you came. You came!" She jumps into his arms and locks her legs around his waist and starts kissing him. He kisses her once and then sets her down.

He keeps looking around as she pulls him over to the side. Then he spots us sitting on the side. He seems to scrutinize each of us like he has X-ray vision. When he gets to Linda, he really checks her out.

"Who's that?" I ask quietly.

"That's Eric Cyrus. They call him Money Train. He's footing the bill for all this. He's the guy who hit the mega lotto right after he graduated from high school a few years ago. He became a multimillionaire overnight."

"I remember hearing about that about five years ago. I always thought it was just an urban legend."

"Nah, it's real."

"So that's Taj's boyfriend, huh?"

"Oh, hell, no, but she would cut off an arm to be the one. I have no idea why he puts up with her drama, but he does. I swear she must have something on him."

I watch as Taj holds on to him the whole time he is here. When he tries to look away or look over to what we're doing, she literally stands in his way so that all he can see is her. He tries to walk away, but she constantly grabs and holds on to him. He eventually forcibly shrugs her off. She moves back and starts pouting.

Magic Man gets us together again. The music comes on and we start dancing. Everything is perfect. Even Taj has her part right. Everyone can see that she's bumping and grinding for Money Train. Midway into the performance she sees he's watching us. She messes up and she starts yelling at us about how we're not doing our job. She rampages and nobody says anything.

Five minutes later Money Train leaves and Taj hurries out behind him. Magic Man tells us to take a ten-minute break. So I'm just sitting listening to the other dancers complain about Taj and all the changes.

As soon as we sit down together I have to speak up. I can't hold it in any longer. "Okay, what the hell was all that?"

"That was Taj the skank on a good day."

I just look at her while the other dancers start laughing and talking about how crazy ass Taj really is. She's usually drunk or high and it's everybody else's job to make her look good. "Just ignore her."

"For real, don't worry about Taj and all her drama. It's how it is sometimes, especially when Money Train is around."

I just shake my head. "It sounds so crazy to me. Nobody needs to put up with all this. I seriously hope the money's good."

"Just do your job and take the money. Pride has nothing to do with this."

"So, Kenisha, who have you worked with?" Pamela asks me.

"This is my first music video. I'm not a professional dancer. Y'all are amazing. I can barely keep up," I say.

"Don't even try it, you definitely keep up," Connie says.

"Better than what's-her-face," Linda adds. They all start laughing. I know they're talking about Taj. It's obvious they're not friends with her.

"Oh, my God, for real," Connie says, rubbing her feet.

"Please don't let that no-dancing fool come back up in here," Donna adds. We all laugh again.

"So how do you know Taj the skank?" Pamela asks.

I laugh. They all call her Taj the skank as if it's her real name. But seriously, it fits her perfectly. "She saw me dance on a YouTube video a friend posted and called me. We have friends in common, but I don't actually know her."

All the dancers start looking at one another. "Are your friends dancers?"

"Kind of. My sister was engaged to Tyrece a while back and we're close with Gayle Harmon. She a—"

"Oh, my God, we know Gayle. I love her."

"I know, right, she is so good."

"Yeah, and she's totally professional."

"So you danced with Gayle?" Pamela asks.

"Not professionally. We just dance and play around down at the studio."

"Which studio?" Pamela asks.

"It's a small place called Freeman—"

"Freeman Dance Studio, oh, yeah, I know Freeman."

"We all know Freeman. Is Ms. Jay still there?"

"Yeah, she's still there at least for the time being. She's having a hard time right now. Unfortunately, the building is falling down on our heads."

Pamela and Linda laugh. "It was falling down when we were dancing there, too, remember?" They slap hands and bump fists.

"You said your sister was engaged to Tyrece," Pamela says. I nod. "Your sister is Jade?"

"Yeah, you know her?"

"Nah, only about her and Tyrece and Taj the skank," Pamela says, shaking her head. "That's really messed up."

"For real, Jade should have kicked Taj the skank's ass," Donna adds.

"What do you mean?" I ask.

"That bitch will steal a wet dream if she thought it would get her what she wants," Connie adds.

"I know that's right."

"Wait, so it's true about Tyrece and Taj the skank?"

Magic Man walks out of his office, clapping his hands to get our attention. "All right, all right, enough resting. Let's get this wrapped up."

We all stand up and get back into position. "Connie, is it true? Was something really going on between Taj and Tyrece?" I ask as we stand up.

She looks at me and nods silently. "Taj says it is. She also says that they're still together on the down low."

"What? How?" I stammer.

Magic Man claps his hands repeatedly. "Connie, Kenisha, let's go. You're still on the clock here."

Shit. I get in line as the music gets ready to start. "Pamela, how long do these rehearsals usually last?" I whisper.

She glances up at the clock. "Probably another hour or so."

"Shit," I mutter to myself as the music starts and we begin again. I know Jade has no idea about any of this and there's no way I'm gonna let Taj make a fool out of her. I need to tell her what I know. An hour later, Taj and Money Train return and Magic Man calls it a wrap. He tells us to meet back here the following day at three o'clock and to be prepared to rehearse a few hours longer. I change into my street sneakers, put on my sweatpants, hoodie and jacket, then leave.

No lie, my body is hurting, my leg muscles are tight, my feet are sore and my head is throbbing. I've never danced so hard in my life. But with everything I still feel good, like I'm a part of something and really doing something special even if it is with Taj the skank.

I still think I'm doing the right thing. It's money and we need it. Then I think about the stupid costume. I don't know what I'm gonna do about that. There's no way I can wear it. My grandmother and Jade would kill me.

We all go outside. It's darker than I thought. "Oh, wait, I forgot to give the paperwork back to Devon," I say.

"Go ahead. We'll wait here for you."

I pull out my cell phone and hurry back upstairs. I text Jade that I'm on my way. Then just as I end the text and I walk into the studio, the first thing I hear is this loud bang and then this muffle of voices. It's dark except for the office lights still on. I don't see Devon or Magic Man, but I see Taj and Money Train.

She's in his face yelling because he won't give her more money. Then all of the sudden the argument turns physical. She pushes him and then slaps him. He turns to walk away. She goes at him again. He grabs her wrists and holds her still. She keeps jerking around. She's screaming and crying and he tells her that she has a problem and needs to get help.

My heart starts racing. I can't believe I'm seeing this. She's crying hysterically now, then she turns and looks out the office window seeing me standing here in the studio. Money Train turns and sees me, too. "What are you looking at? Get out," she yells. I quickly turn around and hurry downstairs.

"You ready?" Pamela asks.

"Yeah, let's get out of here," I say nervously.

Connie and Donna carpooled. Linda, Pamela and I head to the Metro station across the street. We take the same train for the first three stops, then they get off and I'm alone all the way to the end of the line.

By the time I get back to the neighborhood I feel like I'm a sleepwalking zombie. I start walking down the street to my grandmother's house. A block away I see Darien sitting in his car with a few other guys. There's a loud discussion going on, but I can't tell exactly what they're saying, not that I really want to know.

Darien gets out and heads in my direction. I know he's gonna say something to me, but I'm too damn tired to even care, so I just keep walking. He stops and waits. I keep walking past him, so then he walks a few steps behind me. "So you acting all new, like you don't know me now, huh?"

I ignore him. I'm too tired to deal with his stupidity.

"I'm talking to you, Kenisha," he kinda growls, then he grabs my hood and pulls to get my attention.

My head and shoulders jerk back and I stop instantly. I whip around quickly and he has no choice but to let go of my hood or get his arm twisted. He looks surprised, like he didn't expect me to respond. "What do you want?" I snap at him. "You got everything already. You got your stupid trophies back, your freedom, so what could you possibly want with me now?"

"You broke my arm, bitch," he grates out.

"You put your hands on me, bitch," I snap right back,

louder than I expected to. His boys turn around and start looking at us. He glances up and sees them.

"I should kick your ass," he threatens.

My heart jumps, but I'm not going out like that. "We all know what happened the last time you tried that." I hurt Darien once and I can do it again.

He looks down at the big bag on my shoulder. It's heavy and he has no idea what's in it. So he just stands there a second and regroups. "You know you cost me a lot of money with your stupid shit," he almost whispers.

"Oh, please, are you serious?"

"What the hell do you think, yeah, I'm serious. I got people on my back because of your ass."

"Well, maybe if you left my ass alone you wouldn't have people on your back. Now, is that all you got?"

"You screwed up my life," he accuses.

"No, you screwed up your own life and it was done a hell of a long time before I moved here. When we first met I actually thought we'd have a lot in common because our fathers are ex-professional football players and even played on the same NFL team, but I was wrong. We don't have anything in common. You're a spoiled, self-centered brat and you need serious anger management classes."

"You haven't seen me angry yet," he says, stepping up right in my face. "Don't think you really run this neighborhood. You don't. I do."

"Darien, get a life, because this one is quickly running out on you."

He looks back at his boys, but they're not paying attention anymore. "What? Was that a threat?"

"No, it wasn't. It was me seeing what's obvious to everybody but you. There's only one end coming for you and right now it's not a good one. Now, is that all you got, 'cause I'm tired."

He glares at me without speaking. I turn around and start walking. As far as I'm concerned, we're through. Whatever he thinks is between us isn't, and he needs to get that through his thick head. I keep walking down the street to the house. I climb the front steps, unlock the front door and go inside. After resetting the alarm I head to my bedroom. I'm too tired to do anything else.

"Kenisha?" Jade calls out from the next room.

"Yeah, I'm home. Sorry I'm so late. I stayed longer at the dance studio than I expected. Did you get my message?" I say, already having my excuse ready.

"Yeah, I got it. Did you eat?"

"Nah, I'm not hungry. I'm just tired."

Jade comes to my bedroom door. I look up at her from the bed. "Damn, you look like shit," she says. "You know you don't need to be dancing that hard or practicing that much. You look like you can barely hold your head up."

"I know, but it feels good to dance like that. It releases stress."

"Speaking of which, your dad called a couple of times. I covered for you, but you need to call him back tonight."

"I'll text him tomorrow," I say.

"Do me a favor and call him tonight. I promised you would."

I nod. "Sure, okay."

She goes back in her room and closes the door. I don't want to get Jade in the middle of drama between me and my dad, so I pull out my cell and call. He picks up on the second ring. "Hey, Dad, it's me."

"Kenisha, where the hell were you tonight?" he starts.

"At the dance studio," I say, without specifying which one.

"No, you weren't. I spoke with Ms. Jay and she hadn't seen you all afternoon or evening."

"I was in one of the private rooms upstairs. She doesn't go up there a lot. She's usually too busy. Did you talk to her about me working there?" I ask quickly, hoping he'll drop the inquisition. He doesn't.

His lecture starts and this time he has new material. "What would your mother say about you hanging out all hours of the night?" he asks rhetorically, then continues. I lay down on my bed and close my eyes with my phone to my ear. I hear his lecture, but then I feel myself fading fast.

"Kenisha. Kenisha," he repeats.

I startle awake. "Yes, Dad, I'm here," I say quickly.

"Are you listening to me? Did you hear anything I just said to you?" he says angrily. "You didn't hear a damn thing I said."

"I heard you, Dad," I lie, 'cause I really didn't. "Yes, I know you're disappointed with me. I try to—"

"What? Of course I'm not disappointed with you. What in the world makes you think something like that?"

"Well, then, I'm sorry you don't trust me, but—"

"Kenisha, don't say that. Of course I trust you. You're the only person in this world I do trust. I just worry about your safety. You're my baby girl. It's just that living in D.C. is…" he says, then pauses. "Look, just go to bed and get some sleep. You sound tired. I'll call you. We'll talk tomorrow."

"Um, I'm studying for the SATs tomorrow. I'll be in the library, so I'll call you instead of you calling me, okay?"

"Yeah, sure, sounds good. We'll do that. You call me."

All of the sudden it's weird. Now my dad is being all nice to me because I call him on his stuff and give him a guilt trip. "Good night, Dad." I'm just about to end the call when I hear my dad call my name. I don't say anything. I just listen.

"Kenisha, I love you, baby girl."

I hear him, but I don't say anything. I've heard him say the words before, but they don't mean much to me anymore. He never changes. Still, I'm surprised, but I don't say anything. I just wait until he ends the call.

I get up, grab the small bag out of my dance bag. I look at the so-called costume again. It's blatantly salacious and just as bad as it was before. I go to the bathroom and try it on, then look at myself in the mirror. There's no way I can do this. My breasts are out except for the tiny circle in the middle, and if we're doing the routine we practiced all afternoon and evening, there's no way it's gonna stay in place. We might as well just be naked.

I take the thing off and stuff it back in the small bag, then put the bag under my bed. I know nobody checks my stuff or goes through my bedroom, but I hide it, anyway. I guess maybe I'm hiding it from myself. I lie down on my bed a minute, thinking about what I'm doing and everything I have to do coming up. It's a lot and even though I did it today, I'm not sure I can keep it up for the next two weeks. I close my eyes and think about my mom. I don't know what she was doing or what she was going through, but I kinda understand her not telling. Sometimes you need to keep your secrets to yourself.

Fifteen

My World, My Way

kenishi_wa K Lewis
I'm on the edge of this thing and about to jump off. I'm ready. Are you ready for me? 'Cause here I come…
4 May * Like * Comment * Share

The week goes by fast. I'm actually able to juggle school, studying, rehearsals, my dad, my sister, Terrence, my friends and dance class. It's crazy, but I'm working it. So far nobody knows what I'm really doing and I intend to keep it that way, at least for right now. But I'm seriously running out of excuses to disappear for hours at a time. My best excuse is that I'm at the downtown library studying since the one near us burned down. I know I can't use that one forever, but for now…

So it's Friday and this insanity is almost over. I just have another week—that's two days of rehearsals, a dress rehearsal and then the video gets shot the week after that. I can't wait to get paid. I figure I'm gonna get at least five thousand dollars and I can't stop smiling.

I have to deal with Taj's crazy ass and constantly lying to everybody, but I'm okay with it. Seriously, the whole idea of contributing to my mom's hospital bill feels so good. I can't wait to hand over the check to my sister.

So, it's last period, I watch the clock on the wall like I usually do. All my work is done. All the exams are taken, and the final few minutes I'm just sitting around doing nothing. No joke, I can't wait to be out of here today. I'm so tired of being on perpetual hold.

As a matter of fact, there's no real reason to even be in school today. We're not doing anything. There's no school next week. It's spring break and if I see another Disney movie I'm gonna kill somebody. It was a'ight when I was in elementary and even in middle school, but damn, now I'm in the third year of high school. Does it really look like I'm into talking, singing cartoon animals?

For real, I should have stayed home 'cause this is straight up a waste of my time. I tried to talk Jade into letting me stay home today, but she was, like, "no way," and she wasn't budging. She's so headstrong and stubborn. Actually, I'm beginning to think that's a family trait.

So anyway, I don't complain too much. I kinda get it. I know it's mainly because our grandmother is coming home this afternoon and she needs things to look as normal as possible and that means me. So fine, I'm at school today wasting my time sitting in class.

Cassie is sitting right behind me and to the side. She's been quiet all week. But I haven't been on Twitter or Facebook since Monday, so I really don't know what's up. I do know she's hasn't said anything to me and that's all I care about. I'd hate to get kicked out of school because I kicked her ass. So all this means is that I'm seriously not in the mood to deal with drama today. If anything jumps off, I'm just gonna have to step aside and let it pass. I know I have to deal with these fools, but it don't mean I have to be one of them.

So I'm in class and it's dark. The movie's on and half the class is asleep, including the guy next to me who's snoring and drooling like he's been in hibernation for a month. The other half is either talking or texting or plugged in listening to their music. I fall into the last category. Nobody's paying attention, not even the teacher. I guess I can't really call him a teacher. He's a sub. He apparently graduated from the Penn a few years ago and he still knows a few guys here. So they're up there in front at the desk laughing and talking like it's half-time on the football field.

The bell rings. School is done for the day and that means I can leave all that craziness behind me. I get up and head to the door. There are a couple of idiots playing around and that jams us up in a bottleneck. Then somebody pushes them out into the hall. Two guys bump into another two guys and they fall on the floor. This starts a macho shoving match, which quickly turns into stupid drama. I don't wait around to see what happens.

So I'm headed down the hall when I hear my name called. I ignore it and just keep going until I hear it again. This time it's louder and firmer. I know it's my teacher and I can either just keep walking out or I can deal with it. She calls me again.

"Kenisha, wait a minute. I'd like to speak with you."

I turn around. Ms. Grayson is looking at me with this stern expression on her face. "Yes," I say nicely as she goes back into her classroom. I follow, seeing her standing at her desk.

"Kenisha, I need to talk to you about your application to

become a congressional page." She walks from behind her desk and then leans back on the front side.

"I heard the program got cut."

"Yes, it did. After one hundred and eighty-four years Congress agreed to end funding."

"Do you know why? Is it because of all the sex scandals?"

"I think perhaps it has more to do with economics than controversy. At around five million dollars each year, it's probably just too expensive on the taxpayers' dime. Plus, with more advanced technology such as fax machines and the internet, they've dispensed with the need to have messages and files hand delivered. In the end, rising costs trump sentimentality, scandals and history."

"Figures, just when I get ready to step in, they shut it down."

"There are other internship programs available to you in both the political and private sectors. You can do any number of things at this point."

"I know."

"So whatever you decide to do, remember businesses and colleges are looking for students with high achievements and excellent academic records. You need to keep your grades up, be on top of your game and stay focused. Make sure the choices you're making now reflect the consequences you can live with later."

I'm so sick of her always telling me what I need to be doing. But still all I do is nod and repeat, "Yes, I understand. I am."

She shakes her head. "No, not when you're consistently cutting my class. You were out twice this week. You're gonna have to do a lot better than that, Kenisha."

"I have a really good reason, Ms. Grayson. I just can't

say anything about it right now. Can I go now? My grand-mother's coming home today."

She looks at me and nods. "Okay, have a good spring break."

"Bye, Ms. Grayson." I leave her class and head to my locker. As soon as I turn the corner I groan. I really don't need this today. Troy is at his locker and his boys are hanging out, joking around as usual. I expect we're gonna play the stupid game we always play even though he says he's so different. We'll see.

I walk up to my locker and his boys start to leave. They don't say anything to me, they just say goodbye to Troy, then walk away. As soon as they're gone, he turns and looks at me. "Hey," he says.

"Hey." I get to my locker and start spinning the lock. He gets his things and closes his locker. I hear the slam and look over. He steps back to leave. "So what's all that about?" I ask, seeing and hearing his boys exiting the school at the far end of the hallway.

"All what?" he asks.

"No jokes in front of your boys. They just walk away." I open my locker and start putting stuff in, then grab my backpack out.

"Things change," he says, leaning back on the other lockers and looking down the hall as the last few students gather their things for spring break. "Hannah told me she invited you to her birthday party tomorrow."

"Yeah, she did. What time is it?"

"It's a kid's party, so it's around two o'clock."

I smile. "You gonna play pin the tail on the donkey, too?" I joke. He looks at me very seriously. I can't really figure out what he's thinking. Then I guess I must have insulted him. "I was just joking."

"Yeah, I know," he says half smiling.

"Where do you live?"

"I'll send you the address."

"Okay, tell Hannah I'm gonna try to make it."

"She really wants you to come."

I nod. "I'll try."

"I'll tell her." He nods and walks away.

That was odd. I'm not sure what all that was about and right now I don't have time to think with it. My grandmother's coming home today. Jade and I are supposed to be cooking a huge lasagna dinner for her, so I have to get home and help out. She's going shopping and I'm in charge of straightening the house up—which isn't much to do.

I get home and as soon as I open the door I hear laughter in the kitchen. I walk down the hall and get to the kitchen doorway and see Tyrece sitting at the table chilling and Jade putting food away. He smiles with ease and opens his arms to greet me like he always does. "Hey, little sis," he says. "How you been? What's up?"

As soon as I see him sitting there so calmly I instantly think about what the dancers were saying and what Connie confirmed. Tyrece and Taj were still together and he's playing my sister. I step back and just look at him. "What are you doing here?" I say, sounding more hostile than I expect. Both Tyrece and Jade look surprised by my comment. He plays it off, she doesn't.

"Damn, Kenisha," Jade says. "What's with the hostility?" she asks while pulling groceries from another bag.

Tyrece laughs it off, thinking I'm joking with him. "Yeah, I know I haven't been around for a while. But I'm headed overseas next week and I just had to stop by today to see my Jade," he says, smiling at her. She smiles back.

Right then I see it. It's written all over her face—she still loves him. I just shake my head. I never told her what I found out about Tyrece and Taj and I'm not sure if I should now. If I tell her I know she's gonna ask me how I know and I can't tell her the truth—that one of Taj's dancers told me. So I have to find a way to tell her what Tyrece is doing without actually telling her. Right now I guess I just have to play along with his game.

"Sorry, I had a bad day. I guess I'm in a guy-bashing mood." I walk over and start helping Jade put the cereal and canned food away.

"Guy bashing? Why are you guy bashing? What happened?"

I should have known Jade would ask me this question. It's not her getting all up in my business or being nosy. I get that. It's just her being concerned. But actually, I'm thinking this is the perfect opening. I can tell her without really telling her.

"Um, I found out one of my girlfriend's boyfriend is cheating on her. She loves him, but he's playing her," I say, then watch for Tyrece's reaction. He doesn't really have one, at least none I can discern. "I want to tell her, but I got the information how I wasn't supposed to."

"What do you mean?" Jade asks.

"Um, let's say I overheard it someplace where she doesn't know I was and I don't want her to know that part right now. So now, what do I do? Tell her or not?"

Jade comes over to the table where Tyrece is sitting. He holds his hand out to her and she takes it. "That's a hard decision. Not everybody is ready to hear the truth when you think they are, or when you think they should."

"So you're saying don't tell her?"

"I'd wait a while. The truth always comes out in time."

"What about you, Tyrece? What do you think I should do knowing this ass is making a fool of one of my best friends?"

He shakes his head. "Shit like that happens all the time. Dude wants to be a player. Tell her so she can dump his triflin' ass and move on."

"See, that's what I was thinking about doing. But what if she asks how I found out?"

"You have to tell her the whole truth or you'll sound suspect. But in all that telling make damn sure you know what you're talking about."

"Huh?"

"Check your source."

"What do you mean?"

"I mean, shit comes out about me all the time. I'm supposed to be with this girl or that girl. That shit's not true. But still it's out there. You can't be messing up somebody's thing 'cause of something you overheard. Make sure it's true first."

I nod. Yeah, okay, he has a point. But why would Connie lie? But she did say that she heard it from Taj, and she's seriously suspect when it comes to reality. I can definitely see her lying about this. Still…

"So, what you doing dancing with Taj?" Tyrece asks out of the blue.

My heart jumps. Shit, he knows, I'm thinking. I look at Jade, but she's back to putting stuff away. I look back at Tyrece. He's just looking at me, waiting for an answer. "I'm just dancing, no big deal," I say to him.

"I saw the pictures on the Net. You and your girls look good out there. What was it, a frat party?" he asks. I nod. "And I heard she wants you to dance on her next video," he adds. I still don't say anything. "Just say no—trust me, you don't need that kinda drama. You gotta be careful of Taj. She's in this for herself. She'll screw you if she can."

"She already said no," Jade answers for me.

"Good."

"Hello, anybody home?"

The three of us stop and look at one another. I walk over to the kitchen door. I see my grandmother coming in the house. "Grandmom," I say, going to her, "what are you doing here?"

"Well, good gracious, I think I still live here, don't I?" she jokes. Then she opens her arms and I go to her. We hug a long time. I know she's only been gone a week, but for some reason it feels like forever. All of the sudden I know she is my normal, just like Jade is for Tyrece. She's the one person who keeps me focused. So right now I just want to hold on to her and not let go. "I missed you," I say.

"I missed you, too, sweetie." She holds me away and looks into my eyes, then pats my cheek softly. "I missed you, too."

Afterward I step aside as she hugs Jade and then Tyrece. We all start laughing for no real reason. "So what happened?" Jade says. "You're early. You were supposed to come home later this evening. We were planning on picking you up at the station. How'd you get home?"

"I was able to catch that new super-fast train. Good Lord, that thing moves fast. We got here in half the time. Then I grabbed a cab at Union Station. No sense dragging you out into the crazy D.C. traffic. I guess I missed my girls too much."

"We missed you, too," we say, hugging her again.

"I'll take your bags upstairs to your room," Tyrece says, picking up the two pieces of luggage and an extra bag she had with her.

"Oh, no, not that one, Tyrece. That one goes in the kitchen. I brought it back from Georgia just for the girls."

"What is it?" I ask, thinking she brought presents.

Jade, Grandmom and I go into the kitchen. Jade gets her a glass of water and I finish putting the groceries away. Then I grab the small bag. As soon as I open it I smell the sweet aroma of peaches. I pull one out and sniff it. "Mmm, oh, man, this smells so good."

Jade comes over and pulls a peach out of the bag, too. "Oh, it does."

"Now you have to wash them first," Grandmom says. "But, oh, my goodness, they're so juicy and sweet you won't believe it. Your second cousin Jasmine picked them right off the tree early this morning for me."

"Our cousin… I don't think I ever met her," I say.

"If you met Jasmine, you'd remember," Jade says.

"I promised Jasmine she could come up and visit with us this summer. She's excited. She's your age, Kenisha. I told her all about you. She can't wait to meet you."

"Cool, sounds like fun," I say.

Jade chuckles. "I remember Jasmine. That girl stays in trouble—reminds me of someone else." She looks at me, smiling.

"Don't even try it. It's not my fault that stupid things keep happening around me."

Jade laughs. "That's the same thing Jasmine always says. Can you imagine the two of them in the same house?"

"Oh, it's gonna be wonderful," my grandma says happily.

Jade and my grandmother keep talking, but I start wondering about my family in Georgia. My mom never talked about them, so I don't really know much about them. But I do remember her visiting them a few times last year. I didn't want to go, so she went by herself. Now I'm wondering if she actually went or was she in the hospital or something like that.

Jade grabs the bag of peaches and takes them over to the sink to wash. Then she sits them on a few paper towels. My grandmother's still talking about her trip to Georgia and how she spent her week with her sister and her family. She went on and on about her sister's garden and the fruit trees in the backyard.

Tyrece walks into the kitchen. "Hey, I've got a great idea. Why don't I take everybody out to dinner to celebrate?"

"Actually, I'm bone weary from all that traveling today. You all go. I think I'm gonna take me a short nap."

"No, we'll cook here. You can take your nap and when you get up dinner will be ready. What would you like to eat?" Jade says.

"You know, I've been having a taste for smothered pork chops and apple sauce with green beans and macaroni and cheese."

"Mmm, that sounds good," Tyrece says.

"Okay, let's do it. Grandmom, you go take your nap. We have everything covered here," Jade says. Grandmom nods and heads upstairs.

We quickly make a new plan for the dinner menu including some kind of peach dessert. Tyrece goes out to get a few more things from the grocery store. Jade and I get started cooking. An hour and a half later we sit down to a fantastic dinner in the dining room. Afterward we sit around the table laughing, talking and enjoying roasted peaches with amaretti crumble and coffee.

After dinner Jade and Tyrece go out. I clean up the kitchen, then head upstairs, finding my grandmother in her bedroom crocheting. I knock on her open door. She looks up, smiling. "You didn't want to go out with your sister?" she asks.

"Nah, not really in the mood. What are you making?"

"Doilies," she says.

"Could you teach me how to do that one of these days?"

"Sure."

I watch her for a few more minutes, then decide to go to my room. "Do you want anything from the kitchen?"

"No, sweetie, I'm gonna get to bed early."

"Okay, good night, Grandmom," I say.

"Do you want to tell me what's been on your mind all evening?" she says, smiling just like she did when she first saw me and touched my cheek.

"What do you mean?" I ask, trying to look as innocent as possible. Her expression doesn't change. I should have known there's no way to fool her. But I just need a few more days, then everything will be okay. "Nothing's wrong exactly."

"Are you sure?"

"I have a question. What if you have to do something that you know isn't quite right, but you have to do it to help somebody else?"

"Is it something you're gonna be embarrassed about?"

"Maybe."

"Then don't do it," she says simply.

"But what if you don't have a choice?"

"Kenisha, there's always a choice."

"No, not always," I say.

"You still don't do it."

"But what if you have to."

"Kenisha, enough dancing around all this. Tell me what's going on."

"Can I wait and tell you later?"

"I don't know. Can it wait until later?" she asks me.

"I think so. I hope so."

"Kenisha, know this. In all things respect yourself. At all times respect yourself. You're far too old for me to tell you what's right and what's wrong. You already know," she says. I nod. "Okay, good night, Kenisha."

"Good night, Grandmom," I say, then go upstairs to my bedroom. I sit at the window on the top floor like I usually do. I look down on the backyard and think about what I'm doing. See, this is when I need my girls, but I can't tell them, either. So maybe I'll just kind of ask their advice without really asking their advice.

The video shoot is coming fast, and right now I'm about to bust with the news. I need to tell somebody. It's for two days, all day long. There's no way I can just disappear like that without somebody asking something. I need help and I guess it's time to step up and tell my girls. I hit up my Twitter account to see what's up.

sixteen

No New Road—Same Ole, Same Ole

kenishi_wa K Lewis
You'd think I'd get tired of this or at least learn to deal better. Guess not.
4 May * Like * Comment * Share

kenishi_wa K Lewis
@jalisa_jas @diamond_jewels *hey, y'all, what's up? long time, no see/hear/text...* 9 minutes ago

jalisa_jas Jalisa Saunders
@diamond_jewels *who's that?* 9 minutes ago

diamond_jewels Diamond Riggs
@jalisa_jas *i have no idea.* 9 minutes ago

kenishi_wa K Lewis
@jalisa_jas @diamond_jewels *a'ight, y'all can stop playin' now, you know who it is.* 9 minutes ago

diamond_jewels Diamond Riggs
@kenishi_wa *where the hell have you been, girl? haven't talked to you all week.* 9 minutes ago

jalisa_jas Jalisa Saunders
@kenishi_wa *i know, right. where have you been hiding? don't tell us you got some crazy drama going on.* 9 minutes ago

kenishi_wa K Lewis
@jalisa_jas @diamond_jewels *sorry, i've been really busy. no crazy drama—much. how's everybody doing?* 9 minutes ago

diamond_jewels Diamond Riggs
@kenishi_wa *whatever...* 8 minutes ago

jalisa_jas Jalisa Saunders
@kenishi_wa *like you care...* 8 minutes ago

diamond_jewels Diamond Riggs
@jalisa_jas *first she disappears all week and now she's all up in our business.* 8 minutes ago

kenishi_wa K Lewis
@jalisa_jas @diamond_jewels *come on, y'all. i've just been crazy busy dancing.* 8 minutes ago

diamond_jewels Diamond Riggs
@kenishi_wa *smh—i'm fine.* 8 minutes ago

jalisa_jas Jalisa Saunders
@kenishi_wa *yeah, me, too, fine.* 8 minutes ago

kenishi_wa K Lewis
@jalisa_jas @diamond_jewels *y'all going to the dance studio this weekend?* 8 minutes ago

diamond_jewels Diamond Riggs
@kenishi_wa *nah, i don't think i'm going. i have a million things to do.* 7 minutes ago

jalisa_jas Jalisa Saunders
@kenishi_wa *me, neither—i have to work all weekend. so what up? how's working at freeman going?* 7 minutes ago

kenishi_wa K Lewis
@jalisa_jas @diamond_jewels *haven't started yet. hopefully soon. but speaking of dancing I got some news.* 7 minutes ago

diamond_jewels Diamond Riggs
@kenishi_wa *hope it's another frat party—;)* 7 minutes ago

jalisa_jas Jalisa Saunders
@kenishi_wa *ohhh, yeah—i'm there!* 7 minutes ago

kenishi_wa K Lewis
@jalisa_jas @diamond_jewels *nah, it's something better.* 7 minutes ago

jalisa_jas Jalisa Saunders
@kenishi_wa *what's better than last saturday night? for real, that was so much fun. we gotta do that again.* 7 minutes ago

diamond_jewels Diamond Riggs
@kenishi_wa *i know, right—serious good times. i'm in!* 7 minutes ago

kenishi_wa K Lewis
@jalisa_jas @diamond_jewels *trust me—this is seriously better.* 6 minutes ago

jalisa_jas Jalisa Saunders
@kenishi_wa *what is it?* 6 minutes ago

diamond_jewels Diamond Riggs
@kenishi_wa *?* 6 minutes ago

kenishi_wa K Lewis
@jalisa_jas @diamond_jewels *actually, it's too public here. we gotta talk in person.* 6 minutes ago

diamond_jewels Diamond Riggs
@kenishi_wa *can't. I'm carless today.* 6 minutes ago

jalisa_jas Jalisa Saunders
@kenishi_wa *i'm getting dressed. on my way to work right now. what's it about?* 6 minutes ago

kenishi_wa K Lewis
@jalisa_jas @diamond_jewels *it's about the dance job I took.* 6 minutes ago

diamond_jewels Diamond Riggs
@kenishi_wa *what about it?* 6 minutes ago

kenish_wa K Lewis
@jalisa_jas @diamond_jewels *it's not what you think.* 6 minutes ago

diamond_jewels Diamond Riggs
@kenishi_wa *you're making $$$, right? works for me.*
6 minutes ago

jalisa_jas Jalisa Saunders
@kenishi_wa *$$$—me, too.* 6 minutes ago

kenishi_wa K Lewis
@jalisa_jas @diamond_jewels *can y'all skype to-night?* 6 minutes ago

diamond_jewels Diamond Riggs
@kenishi_wa *yeah.* 5 minutes ago

jalisa_jas Jalisa Saunders
@kenishi_wa *yeah.* 5 minutes ago

kenishi_wa K Lewis
@jalisa_jas @diamond_jewels *'k. skype @ 11. so how was school this week? everybody have fun???!* 5 minutes ago

diamond_jewels Diamond Riggs
@kenishi_wa *i think I have senior-itis already. lol.* 5 minutes ago

jalisa_jas Jalisa Saunders
@kenishi_wa *lol—totally agree. but hazelhurst isn't like it was. you got out just in time before all the craziness started.* 5 minutes ago

diamond_jewels Diamond Riggs
@kenishi_wa *for real, exams are kicking my butt plus*

stupid drama stuff everywhere plus studying for the sats. i'm so tired of it all. 5 minutes ago

jalisa_jas Jalisa Saunders
@kenishi_wa *ditto.* 5 minutes ago

kenishi_wa K Lewis
@jalisa_jas @diamond_jewels *i know what you mean.* 5 minutes ago

jalisa_jas Jalisa Saunders
@kenishi_wa *all I think about is being gone from hazelhurst.* 4 minutes ago

kenishi_wa K Lewis
@jalisa_jas @diamond_jewels *if you think hazelhurst is bad, try the penn. assholes everywhere. can't even go to my locker without assholes in my face. lots of bullshit at penn. i just want it over and done with NOW! i'm ready to get out of there. all of the sudden the place is just trifling and the students are trifling-err.* 4 minutes ago

Shit, just as I finish typing, my mention notification beeps again. I check out to see who's trying to talk to me.

Cassie4u Cassie
@kenishi_wa *you talkin' 'bout me again?* 4 minutes ago

Shit. I hurry up and tell Jalisa and Diamond to go look on Cassie's Twitter page. Bitch done lost her mind again.

diamond_jewels Diamond Riggs
@kenishi_wa *what? who is that?* 4 minutes ago

Cassie4u Cassie
@diamond_jewels *mind your business.* 4 minutes
ago

Oh, my God! That bitch is creeping on my page and my
girls' pages, too. WTF!

jalisa_jas Jalisa Saunders
@kenishi_wa *??? wtf.* 4 minutes ago

kenishi_wa K Lewis
@jalisa_jas @diamond_jewels *party line! just ignore
it—i do. it'll go away in a minute.* 3 minutes ago

Cassie4u Cassie
@kenishi_wa *it???!!!* 3 minutes ago

jalisa_jas Jalisa Saunders
@kenishi_wa *wtf?!* 3 minutes ago

diamond_jewels *Diamond Riggs*
@kenishi_wa *who is that?* 3 minutes ago

kenishi_wa K Lewis
@jalisa_jas @diamond_jewels *don't pay attention
to the stupidity. i hear it all the time.* 2 minutes ago

Mya_nomoreBS Mya
@kenishi_wa *omg! you are such a bitch. stupidity!?!*
2 minutes ago

WTF, I got another twatcher on my ass. I know it's Cassie's girl, Mya. What an asshole. I click on Cassie's conversations and see the visual of them tweeting about me. Bitches.

Cassie4u Cassie
@Mya_nomoreBS *wtf. i know that heffer ain't just call me stupid.* 2 minutes ago

Mya_nomoreBS Mya
@Cassie4u *yes, she did.* 2 minutes ago

Cassie4u Cassie
@kenishi_wa *you act all bad and shit. but you just a punkette trying to be something you not. you ain't shit.* 1 minute ago

Mya_nomoreBS Mya
@Cassie4u *roflmao. lol. see, now she ain't got nothing to say to us. you right. she only act all bad when she's got her girls around. smh. lol.* 1 minute ago

kenishi_wa K Lewis
@Cassie4u *seriously, i'm not even talking to you and i don't have beef with you or your younguns. so do me a favor and stay out of my business. what is your problem?!* 1 minute ago

Cassie4u Cassie
@kenishi_wa *my problem is YOU! you always trying to take something that don't belong to you.* 1 minute ago

kenishi_wa K Lewis
@jalisa_jas @diamond_jewels *whatever. jewels/jas, later. too much chatter—i'm out.* 1 minute ago

Cassie4u Cassie
@kenishi_wa *you're such a skanky bitch.* 1 minute ago

kenishi_wa K Lewis
@jalisa_jas @diamond_jewels *skype @ 11.* 1 minute ago

Cassie4u Cassie
@Mya_nomoreBS *see, I told you she was gonna act all innocent as soon as I called her ass out. she always do shit like that. told you. she did gia the same way when she took terrence and then sierra when she took darien.* 1 minute ago

Cassie4u Cassie
@Mya_nomoreBS *now look what's she doing to you. she trying to take your man, too. she think she got everybody fooled cause they think she all nice. i told you i don't buy her shady shit. skank heffer. you need to just jack her ass up.* 1 minute ago

Mya_nomoreBS Mya
@Cassie4u *you think?* 1 minute ago

Cassie4u Cassie
@Mya_nomoreBS *hell, yeah. kick her ass. but i just want to be there when you do. i want to see her hurt bad. So yeah. do it.* 1 minute ago

Mya_nomoreBS Mya
@Cassie4u *yeah. okay. i will. she mess with the wrong bitch this time. i'm gonna kick her ass.* 1 minute ago

So even though I type and tweet in my last words on the subject and decide to let it drop, the tweets keep coming. I don't type anything. They get more and more aggressive and hurtful talking about me. I'm getting more and more pissed off. Cassie and her girl are seriously messing with me and I'm tired of it. I never did anything to her, so I have no idea what her problem is. But stooping to their level with a bunch of Twitter bullshit isn't gonna get them off my back. I need to step up my game and make this public.

Cassie4u Cassie
@Mya_nomoreBS *so when you gonna do it?* 1 minute ago

Mya_nomoreBS Mya
@Cassie4u *i don't know. when do you think I should?* 1 minute ago

Cassie4u Cassie
@Mya_nomoreBS *as soon as possible. when we go back to school after spring break. everybody needs to see this. don't worry, i got your back.* 1 minute ago

Mya_nomoreBS Mya
@Cassie4u *bet.* 1 minute ago

All right, enough of this bullshit, I'm not going down like this. I shadow in the tweet conversation including Cassie's part and then press the copy key. I drop the text down on a white document page and then create a file. Six pages of mostly bullshit appear on screen.

I look at the printed pages and then read it over. I'm tired of dealing with these fools and I'm not playing their game anymore. They're all cowards dressed like bullies hiding in cyberspace and I don't have any more time for this stupid shit. In the span of nine minutes my mood changes from hooking up with friends and feeling good to totally pissed off. I don't know what's wrong with some people. They just need to get their drama off any way they can. "Enough of this stupid stuff," I say, then turn my phone off.

seventeen

Unstill Waters

kenishi_wa K Lewis
It's all nice and calm on the surface, but that's all for show. Beneath, there's mud and rocks and it's a lot deeper than it appears. Diving in headfirst can be a mistake... Splash.
5 May * Like * Comment * Share

shit. I fell asleep last night and missed Skyping with my girls. I also missed the eight text messages, four emails and two phone calls—all from Jalisa and Diamond. Plus I missed a text message and phone call from Terrence. I guess I was just plain tired. So I wake up early Saturday morning knowing that I have a crazy day ahead of me. I shower, dress and head downstairs. My grandmother is already in the kitchen. She's drinking her coffee and reading the newspaper. "Good morning, Grandmom."

"Good morning. I see you're ready for your run," she says.

"Yep," I say, grabbing a water bottle from the refrigerator. "I'll be back in about an hour or so."

"Okay, be safe."

"I will. See you later." I leave out the back door. I stretch, then turn on my music and put in my earbuds. I walk around to the front of the house, then down the path to the sidewalk. I look around. The street is empty except for a few people walking their dogs and someone rolling a shopping cart. I turn toward my usual route and start running. As soon as I get half a block I remember why I love doing this. It feels great to be out in the fresh air feeling my heart beat faster and faster. Fifteen minutes later I'm on a roll. My breathing is paced and my stride is long and steady.

I get to a traffic light and stop, but still keep running in place. The music I'm listening to is fast paced and I keep running to the beat. A few seconds later someone comes up beside me. They don't say anything and I don't look to see who it is, but the first thing I think is it's Darien. My heart jumps, then races. I get ready to run and dash in between the moving cars. Then I hear my name. I pull an earbud out and turn, seeing Terrence running in place beside me. I smile instantly. "Hey, what are you doing here?"

"Is that the greeting I get?"

I stop running and throw my arms around his neck and hug him hard. "You scared me."

"Scared you?" he repeats, questioning.

"Yeah, I didn't expect to see you. I'm glad you're here. I didn't know your were coming home this weekend."

"I called to tell you last night, but when you didn't pick up I decided to just surprise you. I saw you running."

The light changes and we walk across the street, then on the other side we start running again. As we run we're talking about our plans for the day. He's gonna do some tutoring and then get back to mowing a few lawns in the neighborhood. I told him about the birthday party I was invited to, but didn't add that Troy would be there.

"Do you want company?" he asks.

I start laughing. "Okay, now, can you really see yourself at an all-girls birthday party with, like, fifteen or sixteen eleven-year-olds running around? Nah, that's okay. Somehow I can't see that happening."

He laughs, too. "Are you sure?" he asks.

"Yeah, I'm sure. Why don't we catch up afterward? I'm gonna head over to Freeman, then go to my dad's place."

He nods. "Okay, sounds good. I'll meet you at Freeman."

We finish our run and head back to my grandmother's house. We walk up to the front porch and stand there a minute. "You okay?" he asks.

"Yeah, why?"

"I don't know. You seem kind of off today. Then last night you didn't answer your cell phone."

"I turned it off."

He looks at me. "Seriously, you turned it off. I didn't know that was possible. Aren't you, like, addicted to your cell?"

"No, I'm not addicted to my cell phone," I say, swatting his arm and missing because he moves away quickly. He heads back down the front path, waving. "See you later."

I go back inside and start my day. My grandmother heads to one of her seniors' church group meetings and then to bingo. I do some homework and catch up on studying for my SATs. I take a break and leave text messages and voice messages to Jalisa and Diamond, but since both of them have to work today, I assume they're already at their jobs. So I get back to homework and studying. After a while studying word meaning and taking practice SAT tests online gets monotonous and I guess I fall asleep. I wake up when my cell phone rings. I grab it fast. "Hello."

"Kenisha."

"Hi, Dad," I say, still a little groggy.

"Are you okay?"

"Yeah, I guess I fell asleep while I was studying."

"Is your grandmother home?"

"I don't think she's home right now, but she's home from Georgia. She got back yesterday when I got home from school."

"Good. I spoke with your dance instructor yesterday. I agreed that it was okay for you to work there on weekends only. I don't want this job interfering with your school work."

I start smiling. This is the best news I've heard in a long time. "Thanks, Dad. I'm going over later, so maybe I can start today."

"One more thing. Courtney wants you to come over to the house for dinner. She's planning a family meal this evening."

"What?" I say, totally stunned.

"She's been cooking all day, so I think it would be a good idea for you to come."

"Dad, I can't. I already have plans for tonight." The idea of eating food that Courtney cooked is revolting. She can't cook tap water. And if I know her, and I do, she'll probably try to poison my food and then blame it on me.

"Kenisha, whatever plans you have for this evening, change them. This is more important. Courtney's going through a lot of trouble to do this for you. She's trying to make this work and you need to do your part and support her."

Okay, seriously, I have no idea what this is all about, but I know it ain't about being friends. I know Courtney and she doesn't just roll over and be nice to me. She's up to something and it probably has to do with me getting into trouble so that she makes me look bad to get money from my father. "Are you going to be there tonight or are you going out?" I ask.

"What do you mean? What kind of question is that? Of course I'm gonna be here this evening. It's Saturday night with the family," he says indignantly, then continues. "You need to change your attitude...."

I almost laugh out loud. I can't believe he just said that, and to act like he's all offended is just way too over the top. For real, it's a valid question given my father's actions. He's never home on Saturday evenings. He doesn't even know what a Saturday night at home with the family looks like. So chances are he's gonna find a way to slip out and do his thing, anyway.

"...so like it or not this is it. We're a family, Kenisha, and you're a part of it. I think it's about time you start acting like you are, understand?"

Okay, I have no idea what he's been smoking, sticking or snorting, but all this "we're a family" is total bullshit. We're not a family.

"Do you hear me?" he says louder.

"Yes, I hear you. Can I bring Terrence with me?" I ask.

"What part of 'family' do you not understand?" he asks rhetorically, then pauses a few seconds. "Look, I know you and Courtney have had your problems in the past, but if she's willing to make amends and meet you halfway I don't see why you can't do the same."

I don't say anything. After a while he gets it.

"Are you still there?"

"Yes."

"This isn't a request, Kenisha. I insist you come."

"What time?" I ask.

"Seven o'clock."

"Fine, is that it?" I ask resentfully.

"Yes, and be on time, please."

"Bye," I barely mutter, and then end the call.

I change my clothes, pack and grab my dance bag, then head out. As soon as I lock the door behind me and step outside on the porch I see Li'l T across the street hanging with his friends. I don't bother saying anything to him. I just start walking. Actually, I have nothing to say. He took the video down from YouTube, but now it's everywhere else, so whatever. He shouldn't have made in the first place, but it's too late for all that.

Out of the corner of my eye I see one of his boys hit his arm and nod over to where I'm walking. He turns and yells across the street, then comes over. "Perfect timing," he says. "I was just coming to see you. I've got some news and you're gonna—"

"I don't have time to play with you," I abruptly interrupt.

"Aw, see, why you gonna be like that? I was just trying to tell you about your boy Darien."

"You can stop right there. I don't even want to know."

"I'ma tell you, anyway. I heard his boys are supposed to be after his ass—he owes them a lot of money and he ain't got it. They're gonna kick his ass when they find him."

"When they find him," I repeat.

He chuckles. "Yeah, he's all of the sudden nowhere around."

"Whatever," I say, then my cell phone rings, thank God.

I pull it out and answer. At this point I really don't care who it is. "Hello."

"Kenisha."

"Yeah, who's this?"

"It's Hannah. Are you coming to my birthday party today?"

I have to stop a second and think. Then I glance at my phone to check the time. Its twenty minutes after two and I guess I'm already late. I forgot all about her birthday party. So my first thought now is to say no, but I can tell she really wants me to come. "Um, yeah, sure, but just for a little while, okay? I have to practice. Has it started yet?"

"Uh-huh."

"Okay, what's your address?"

"Troy can pick you up and drive you. Here, hold on…"

"No, wait, that's okay. Just give me your address," I say. Then I hear Troy's deep voice in the background and a muffling sound. Apparently Hannah is giving him the phone. "Hey, it's Troy. I need your address."

I don't say anything at first. Li'l T is still walking beside me. He's pretending like he's not interested in my conversation, but I know he is. He's the biggest gossip in the neighborhood. I can just see Troy picking me up and him telling everybody, including Terrence. "No, that's okay. I can get there."

"Actually, you can save me from all this pink craziness. It's like a bottle of Pepto-Bismol exploded up in here. I need to serious cut out for a while, so let me pick you up, please."

I have to smile. I can just see him surrounded by a bunch of ten- and eleven-year-olds all dressed in pink. "All right, meet me at Freeman."

"Okay, I'll be there in fifteen minutes."

We hang up and a second later Li'l T is right on me. "So, what up with you and my man Troy?" he says.

"What?" I say, totally surprised.

"I thought you were kicking it with T?"

"I am, so don't be starting any mess. Do you understand?"

"Yeah, yeah, I'm good. I'm just asking, that's all," he says, "because T's my boy and you're my girl and all. I just don't want to see all that get messed up with Troy."

"Look, I'm going to Troy's sister's birthday party. Terrence knows all about it. So drop it."

"A'ight, a'ight, I'm just lookin' out."

"Goodbye, Jerome," I say, using his real name like I do when he gets on my nerves and I've had enough of him.

"A'ight, see you later—oh, wait, one more thing. So what's up with Troy's sister? She cute or what?" he asks, interested.

I smile playfully. "Yeah, she's cute. She's really cute—and she dances, too."

"Really," he says with added interest, "so a'ight, a'ight, why don't you do me a favor and hook a brotha up." He leans in closer as if to whisper, "You know, get me those digits."

"All right, I will. How about in another ten years."

"Ten years, why ten years?" he asks.

"'Cause today's her birthday—she's eleven," I say nicely. He jerks back and scrunches his face up. "What!"

I start laughing 'cause his expression is just too funny.

"I see you got big jokes, huh—not funny," he proclaims.

I just keep laughing, then watch him shake his head as he ignores me and hurries down the street calling after two girls. I can hear them telling him to go away. I shake my head. Li'l T will never change. I sit down on Freeman's front steps to wait. My cell phone rings. I see that it's Jalisa and answer. "Hey, girl, what's up? I thought you have to go to work today."

"Hey, yeah, I do, but not until later. Diamond's working just about all day long today and tomorrow. She wants the extra cash. Her mom's taking her on some college tours next week. So what happened to you last night?"

"I know. I missed the Skype. I turned my phone off and fell asleep. I guess I was more tired than I thought."

"No, uh-uh—I'm not buying that. You've been tired a whole lot lately. Seriously, Keni, what's up with you? You don't want to hang out and barely even talk on the phone. And now you're not even Skyping with us anymore. You're like a whole other person. I know you're not working at Freeman yet, so don't tell me that. What's up? What's going on?"

I consider for a split second telling her what's going on, then quickly decide against it. The last thing I want to hear is a lecture from Jalisa. She's my girl and all, but she can be an I-told-you-so know-it-all sometimes. "For real, Jalisa, it's nothing. I'm just tired."

"I told you I'm not buying that, so don't tell me it's nothing, because I know something's up. Please, I've seen these signs before with my brother Brian. I couldn't stop him, but I'm not letting you go out like that."

All of a sudden it makes sense. She's on my case so hard because she thinks I'm doing drugs like her older brother, Brian. "Jalisa, for real, I'm fine. I'm just—"

"I was too young to help Brian," she interrupts as emotion thickens her voice, "but not now. I can help you now."

"Jalisa, I'm not doing drugs, I swear. You know me. I

don't do stupid stuff like that." She doesn't say anything for a while. I'm thinking she didn't hear me. Then I barely hear her speak.

"Yeah, I thought I knew my brother, too."

"Okay, the truth is I'm tired because I'm not sleeping very well at night."

"Why aren't you sleeping?" she asks.

"I've been having nightmares about my mom." It's the truth. I *have* been having nightmares, but of course it's not the whole truth exactly.

"What kind of nightmare?"

"It's not like I wake up screaming or anything like that. It's just that she's on my mind a lot now. In the dreams it's like she's trying to tell me something."

"What?" she asks.

"I don't know. I never figure it out. But for real, other than not sleeping and the nightmares, I'm fine."

"Okay. So what was all that about last night on Twitter? What is up with your girl Cassie? That was her on Twitter last night, right? She's hating all over you."

"I know. She's totally childish and now she's got this silly ninth grade groupie hanging on her like her fake gold jewelry."

We laugh. "So she just gonna act like a fool until somebody smacks her ass down."

"Yeah, pretty much."

"So what are you gonna do?"

"I made a hard copy of the Twitter conversation from last night. Since she actually threatened me, I'm gonna give it to one of my teachers. She'll know what to do with it."

"All right, as long as you got this."

"I do," I say, seeing Troy's car turn the corner and drive

down the block toward the building. "Listen, I have to get ready to go. I'm on my way to an eleven-year-old's birthday party."

"A what?"

"Do you remember Hannah from the dance studio the other day? She's the kid I introduced to you and Diamond."

"Yeah, I remember her."

"Well, she invited me to her birthday party and I promised I'd go. Her brother is picking me up."

"Who's her brother—is he cute?"

"Yeah, very. It's Troy. You remember him from LaVon's party a few months ago."

"Oh, yeah, I remember him. He is cute. So..."

"Before you even start something, don't. I'm just doing this to be nice to Hannah, his sister."

"I didn't say anything, did I?"

Troy's car pulls up in front of the building and I start walking over. "No, you didn't. But just in case. Okay, I gotta go. I'll tell you all about it later. See ya."

Troy gets out of the car and comes around to the passenger's side. He opens the door for me. I get in and wait until he gets back to the driver's seat. As soon as he does he pulls off. At the first traffic light he stops and looks over to me. "Are you sure you're ready for this?"

I start chuckling. "Come on, it can't be that bad," I say.

He starts laughing. "Oh, believe me. It's even worse than that."

Eighteen

The Path Divides

kenishi_wa K Lewis
I heard it so many times before. The wrong thing done for the right reason is still the wrong thing. I still don't know if it's true. It's probably just bullshit like everything else.
5 May * Like * Comment * Share

We drive down Sixteenth Street northwest past U Street, Howard University and a couple of embassies, headed toward Rock Creek Park. Then we make a turnoff onto one of those small streets with the huge old houses. We keep going for a few blocks, then stop and park in front of one of the smaller houses on a street.

I get out of the car and look around. The neighborhood is nice. It's old with big thick trees that look like they've been standing around here for centuries. The houses are mostly stone and brick and each one is very different. Some are old and some are super modern. It's quiet like my dad's neighborhood, but also there's a constant hum of something in the background. I don't know if it's traffic from the main street or maybe from Rock Creek Park.

"This way," Troy says, and starts walking down the street.

There are cars everywhere. Then we turn the corner and come to this big modern-looking house in the middle of the block. Troy turns to walk up the circular driveway. I follow. But instead of going to the front door he leads me around back. I can hear the laughter and loud music as we get closer. He opens the gate and we go in.

And, oh, my God, Troy was so right. I see exactly what he meant earlier about being surrounded by pink. The house and backyard is decorated in every shade of pink imaginable—from gentle blush to deep hot magenta. Even the pool water is tinted pink. I start laughing. Troy leans over. He's laughing, too. "See. I told you. Pink."

I nod my head. "Yeah, it's definitely pink."

The yard is huge and it's packed. Every kid in the school must have come. We walk around for a few minutes. Troy introduces me to his parents and a few other relatives, one who looks like an older version of Regan, so I assume they're related. Then I hear my name and turn around. "Kenisha, you came."

I turn and see Hannah coming toward me with what looks like a major entourage. She's dressed in pink, of course, with a tiara on her head. "Hey, happy birthday," I say, and give her a hug. "You look great."

She smiles and introduces me to her friends. There are about eight names. She says them in a singsong tone like she's been saying them all her life. They smile and laugh, then leave in the same mass movement in which they came. I just shake my head. I had all kinds of parties all the time, but I seriously don't remember this when I was growing up.

But for real, the party is too over the top. There's a DJ on a platform spinning and some dancers pumping the crowd up. There are two professional photographers roaming the area taking candid shots. There's a fully catered food bar with everything imaginable including chef and servers. There's a mountain of presents piled high and at least two hundred teens, tweens and preteens running around. It's loud and crazy and I already know I'm not staying long.

I grab something to eat, then just kick it with some of the older teens there. A few of them I know from Hazelhurst. So we're standing around talking and then Troy comes over and grabs my hand and starts pulling me. "Come on, I need your help," he says.

Okay, I look at him like he's crazy, but then I go with him, anyway. I have no idea what he's talking about but then we get over to the area set aside for badminton and there's a couple already there waiting. "Uh-uh, no way. I'm not about to be running around after a birdie." I turn to walk back toward the covered patio area, but he grabs my hand again.

"Come on, please. I've been challenged. You can't let me go out like that, can you?"

"All right, fine—one game only," I say definitively.

Six games later we're all still laughing, talking trash and having fun. We take a break and grab some water. I look up and see Regan is there. I have no idea when she arrived, but as soon as we see each other, I know it's time for me go. There's no way I'm gonna be in the same place at the same time with her. I say goodbye to Hannah and Troy's parents, then I get Troy to drop me back off at Freeman. "You know, if you're leaving because Regan showed up, you don't have to. She's not gonna do anything."

"Regan's family, I'm not. Either way it doesn't matter. I already told Hannah I couldn't stay long. She knows that I have to go to dance."

"Did you have a good time?"

"Yeah, it was a lot of fun. Hannah's gonna remember her birthday party forever. Do your parents go all out like that every year?"

"Yeah, mostly," he says.

"For your birthday, too?" I ask. "Do you have, like, baby-blue birthday parties?"

He smiles. "Nah, they gave up on that a while ago. I'm glad you could come, but I'm sorry you're leaving so early," he says as he pulls up in front of Freeman.

I open the door and turn to him. "I glad I came, too. I had fun, but duty calls."

"So what are you doing over spring break?"

"Working."

"Where?"

"Here," I say, turning to look up at the Freeman build-ing. "I'm a dance instructor."

He nods. "Yeah, that's what's up. I can see that."

"A'ight, I gotta go. Thanks again for the ride."

"You're welcome."

I turn and look over at him one more time. For a split sec-ond I actually think about kissing him. But that goes away fast. I just wave and get out of the car and hurry up the front steps. As soon as I get inside I go directly to the office. Ms. Jay isn't there, so I look around the first floor and see she's teaching a ballet class. There's no way I'm gonna interrupt the class to get the key to the auditorium, so I decide to go upstairs to one of the private studios. Hopefully the doors are unlocked.

They are. I go inside and sit down on the windowsill like I usually do. I settle down and get comfortable. I put my earbuds in to listen to my music. I plug in and shuffle some old tunes. First it's Black Eyed Peas' *I Got a Feeling*. I smile and start nodding my head to the beat. Right now this is my favorite place to be. I look down. From the window I can see everything perfectly. Why can't my life be like this all the time?

I start thinking about my day with Troy. I had a great time. Hanging out with him was fun and easy. He's nothing like I thought he was. I don't know why he puts on this act as being someone else. I laugh, thinking about him diving on the ground in an attempt to hit the birdie with his racket. He hit it straight up in the air and then I slammed it over the net right between our opponents. They both missed it. We won the game and we laughed the whole time.

After a while the song changes to something just as old. It's Alicia Keys and Jay-Z's *Empire State of Mind*. I love this song. I'm not from New York, but it makes me just as proud of my own hometown. I lean my head back against the side wall and close my eyes, feeling the lyrics as he raps and she sings. Halfway through the song my phone rings and the song automatically mutes and pauses. "Hello."

"Hello, Kenisha, it's Ms. Jay at Freeman Dance Studio. Will you be coming in today?"

"Hi, Ms. Jay. Yes, I'm already here. I saw you in class earlier and I didn't want to disturb you to get the auditorium door key, so I just came upstairs. I'm in one of the private studios."

"Perfect. Can you meet me in my office?"

"Sure, okay, I'm on my way."

A few minutes later I knock on the frame of Ms. Jay's open office door. She looks up and smiles. "Hi, Kenisha, what do you think about starting work? I could use you in the intermediate hip-hop class today."

"Sure. When does it start?"

She looks at her watch. "In about twenty minutes."

"Okay, I can do that," I say.

"I want you to make sure they stretch before class. Do you remember the routine you did for the summer revival two years ago?"

"You mean that *Nothin' on You* song by B.o.B.? That one?"

"Yes. Do you remember the routine?"

"Uh-huh, but can't I teach them something more current?"

"Let's stick with that one first and then we can work out some new routines for the class."

I nod. "Okay, I'll go change my clothes and stretch. Can I meet them in the auditorium instead of the classroom?"

She looks puzzled, but agrees, anyway. "Sure. Fine, I'll let them know. Make sure you stop by the office before you leave for the day. I have some paperwork for you to complete."

"Okay, I will."

She goes in her drawer and pulls out the auditorium key and gives it to me. "Have a good class."

"I will. Thanks again, Ms. Jay." I go straight to the auditorium. I set the music up, stretch and then get ready for the class to come in. I'm tense and nervous as I go through the *Nothin' on You* routine. I remember it perfectly.

A few minutes later the class arrives. They come down to the front of the stage. They're all rowdy and loud and that's just perfect. I want them to have the energy when they dance. I reset the music and do the routine without saying anything to them. When I finish they all applaud and cheer. Then I tell them I'm gonna teach them how to do it. They really get excited. They stretch and we get started. All the nervousness I felt before is gone. I can't believe this is my first real class as a working teacher getting paid.

The class is over so fast. The young dancers are too excited to come back and I can't wait to come up with some new routines for them. But right now I'm still pumped. Instead of leaving I turn on my music and do my routine. I only get to go through it a couple of times when I see someone walking down toward the stage. I stop dancing and put my hands on my hips. "Shit, not again," I mutter, and then call out to Li'l T 'cause I know that's who it is. "I swear, Jerome, I'm gonna strangle you this time."

"It's not Jerome, it's me."

The person keeps walking and now I see who it is. "Taj, is that you?" I say, still breathing hard from dancing. She keeps walking toward the stage. Now she's applauding. I go down the front steps and meet her as she approaches. She looks completely different, like a normal person. She has on baggy pants and a T-shirt and her hair pulled back in a ponytail with a cap. She's also wearing sneakers, making her even shorter than I thought before. "What are you doing here?"

"They told me this is where you hang out and dance." She looks around with her nose up in the air. "This place is old. It looks like it's about to collapse."

"Yeah, it is old. It's got a lot of history in the neighborhood," I say, still catching my breath from earlier.

"I've always seen it before. It's all big and ugly, but I've never been inside." She looks around again.

"It's pretty bad sometimes. The lights go out because the electricity is bad and the roof constantly leaks when it rains."

"I can see that. It looks like it should be condemned."

"Actually, they're having a dance show to raise money for it. You know, you should think about being a judge for the contest."

"A judge."

"Yeah, like a celebrity judge. We're gonna have the press here to promote it and everything."

"Maybe, I'll think about it."

"So why are you here?" I repeat.

She does that fake smile. "Damn, girl, you're really good up there. I see why you're all over the internet."

"Thanks," I say. "So what's up?"

"Um, I came here because I think we need to talk to clear the air between us," she says, sitting down in the front row. I walk over and sit down, too, leaving an open seat between us. "You don't know me and I don't know you, but I hope we can maybe be friends one day. I don't have a lot of friends. And believe me, I'm not the bitch everybody thinks I am. I'm just trying to do a job in a very hard profession. Nobody gives you a break, so you have to get them yourself any way you can."

"Yeah, but how long can you do that?" I ask her.

"For as long as I have to. It's a hard, rocky climb to the top and I have every intention of getting there. If some people fall along the way, I'm sorry, but I can't carry everyone."

She's kinda cold-blooded, but nothing I haven't seen or heard before. If she were a guy I guess they would call what she has ambition and determination, but being a girl makes her a bitch. Maybe she is just misunderstood and everything is all for the stage persona that Jade talked about before.

"Anyway, I came to apologize. I'm sorry about what happened at the party the other night. I hear I was pretty bad. For real, I'm usually not like that. I'd been drinking and taking anxiety pills to calm me down in order to perform. I guess I get a little flirtatious when the two mix. I hope you didn't take that personally. I remember Terrence from the old days. He's a good friend. He's got that bad-boy thing going on, but he's really a good guy. So, what's he doing these days?"

"He's at Howard University."

She smiles and nods. "I always knew he was gonna do something with his life. Not like some of the other guys in the hood."

"You mean like Darien?"

She looks stunned. "You know Darien?"

"Yeah, kinda."

She shakes her head. "That's a name I haven't heard in a long time. What's he up to?"

"Jail, hopefully," I say.

She laughs. "Yeah, he's a bad boy all the way."

She has this smile on her face like now. "Definitely."

"So, I hear you're Jade's sister—is that right?"

I just nod 'cause I have no idea where she's going with this. She's trying to act all nice, but there's something about her that's just too fake.

"She's nice. I like Jade, but I think she hates me because she thinks I'm on Tyrece or trying to take him from her."

"Are you?"

"No. Hell, no. I don't do stuff like that. Besides, I can have just about any man I want. Tyrece is irrelevant compared to some of the guys out there."

"You mean like the guy at the studio the other day."

"Money Train, yeah, like him. His pockets are really

deep. You know he hit the lotto a few years back and now he spends all his money on me."

"So you're telling me nothing happened between you and Tyrece."

"We're just good friends," she confesses too easily.

"Still," I say, not buying it.

"Yeah, still. All that other stuff was for publicity. We both had CDs to sell and promote. Controversy is the best marketing tool. So, none of that was anything. It's just a lot of noise to sell CDs. I'm surprised Jade didn't get that. But you'll understand all this better once you're in the business longer. It's all about the show," she tells me.

"I don't have to worry about that. I'm not gonna be in the business much longer."

"Why is that?" she asks.

"I'm only doing it because I need money fast," I say.

"Are you pregnant?"

"No," I say indignantly.

"Well, this is what I do and what I always wanted to do. I dropped out of high school," she says proudly. "You know you basically learn everything you need to know already. But you should really consider being a professional dancer. You could be good at it. Of course, you can't dance and go to school. It's the dedication of the craft. You need to do this full-time and quit school."

"I'm not quitting school."

"Then you're not serious about your future. Opportunities like dancing in my video don't come around every day. You need to recognize and appreciate what I'm doing for you. You all do." She shakes her head. "I have to get new dancers every video because nobody gets this. And when

I go on tour I practically have to get new dancers in every city. Nobody takes this seriously."

I can hear the arrogance in her voice. It sounds like the old Taj, the skank, is back. "I dance because I like to and because I can and I'm good at it. Right now I need the money to help pay some bills, that's all."

"How much are the bills?"

"Way too much," I say.

"I know what that's like. Listen, don't worry, I got your back on this."

"Thanks. I didn't tell anybody I was doing this so..."

"You didn't even tell Terrence about doing my video?" she questions and smiles.

"No. Nobody knows."

"What would he say?"

"Nothing he can say. I'm just doing this for the money and I'd appreciate it if you didn't say anything to anybody."

"I told you, I got your back. So anyway, I gotta go now. You get back to dancing. I'll see you next week."

"Okay, see ya," I say, then stand and watch her leave.

I go back on stage, but I don't dance. I'm through. I lock the sound system and grab my stuff to leave. I'm thinking, maybe Taj the skank isn't as bad as they say, after all. She's got my back. I turn off the lights, then take the key back to the office. I get the papers I'm supposed to fill out, then get my work schedule and leave. I glance down the hall and see Taj is still here and she's not alone. She's talking to Terrence. My heart jumps. She has her hand on his arm, pulling him close. She's smiling up in his face and he's smiling back at her.

I'm just standing here watching this. A few minutes later they go outside. I follow. I stand on the steps and see him walking her to a car. He opens the door and she gives him a hug, then gets in. He bends down and they talk some more. I turn around and go home. I've seen enough.

As soon as I get home and go up to my bedroom I hear the doorbell ring. I just let it. I know who it is—Terrence. I don't want to deal with him right now.

Nineteen

Too Little. Too Late.

kenishi_wa K Lewis
How long to realize that when you ignore someone all their life, trying to take control all of a sudden just ain't gonna happen. Get it?
6 May * Like * Comment * Share

Okay, I'm not in the greatest mood right now and sitting here looking at this mess called food is making it worse. So dinner at my dad's house is exactly as I expect—a huge waste of time. For real, I'm not even gonna get into what Courtney cooked mainly because I have no idea what the hell it is.

It's ground beef something and I think it's supposed to be Italian, but after that, who knows. It's red, but not like a spaghetti sauce or marinara sauce—it's like dark bloodred, almost burgundy. I don't eat it. The boys don't eat it and my dad doesn't eat it. So it just sits there as Courtney feeds the baby. She's eating strained peas and squash and everybody's drooling over the baby's food. Of course Courtney's pissed. She's been grumbling for the past twenty minutes.

"Kenisha, why don't you take some more food?" my dad says.

I scrunch up my nose. Right now I have the top part of burned rolls and tart lemonade. "No way?"

"Yes," he says, "just put some on your plate."

I look at the mess sitting in the middle of the table in front of me. It would almost be comical if it wasn't so damn disgusting. "I'm not hungry."

"Me, either," Jr. says.

"Me, either, too," Jason adds.

"Come on, you've always liked spaghetti, right?"

"It's not spaghetti. It's lasagna," Courtney says abruptly, obviously insulted. "Can't you tell the difference?"

"Apparently *you* can't. There's no way that's supposed to be lasagna." I start chuckling. "How did you get the ricotta cheese to turn burgundy?" The boys start laughing, too.

"I don't need this shit," Courtney says, slamming her glass of wine down and breaking the stem. It spills over and she gets up and storms into the kitchen. My dad follows.

"Thank God," I mutter, and stand to leave.

"Thank God," Jr. repeats.

"Yeah, thank God," Jason adds.

An argument starts in the kitchen. "Come on, guys," I say to my brothers, "let's watch some television." The boys follow me to the family room. I pop in a DVD and we sit down to watch. A few minutes later Jr. gets up and Jason follows. They go to the front window and look out. Seconds later they come back to the family room dancing and singing excitedly.

"Jade is here. Jade is here…" they repeat over and over again while running through the house to the kitchen. I get up and go to the front door. They're right. I see my sister's car parked out front. She gets out and walks toward the house. I'm so glad to see her. "Hey, what are you doing here?" I ask, hugging her and then ushering her inside.

"Your dad asked me to come."

"I hope not for dinner," I joke.

"No," Dad says.

We turn around. My dad is walking toward us. Courtney is right behind him. "Thanks for coming, Jade. Come, we need to talk." He heads to his office. "You, too, Kenisha."

We get to the office and go inside. Courtney follows just as my dad is closing the door. "Wait," she says.

"Courtney, I need to speak with Kenisha and Jade alone."

"About what?" she demands.

"This doesn't concern you," he says. She looks at us. Of course I'm smiling.

"If it's in my house, then it concerns me," she says.

"Please, Courtney, it's about their mother." I stop smiling. He closes the door and tells us to have a seat. We sit down on the sofa and wait.

"What about Mom?" I immediately ask.

"Okay, I know you've been asking questions about your mother—what was going on with her. Your grandmother and I talked. We think it's best if you know the truth. I asked her to allow me to tell you."

"Was she sick?" Jade asks, getting right to the point.

He looks at her and nods. "Yes. She was very sick."

"What was it?" I ask him, almost scared to hear his answer.

"Barbara had a virus of the heart."

"A virus of the heart," Jade repeats.

"What does that mean?" I ask.

"She had a very serious viral infection called cardiomyopathy. It went undetected for a long time, so we don't know how long she had the disease. By the time we found out what was wrong it was too late. Ultimately she needed a heart transplant."

Jade and I go silent for a long time. We're just staring into space. How do you process something like this? I'm not sure I can wrap my head around it.

"How did she get it?" Jade asks quietly.

"We don't know."

"Maybe it's genetic... We could have it, too," I say.

"No, no, God, no," he says almost painfully. "That was the first thing she said she found out. You're both fine. Trust me."

"And Grandmom?"

He nods. "She's fine, too."

"You said she needed a transplant. Was she on a donor list or something like that?"

"Yes, she was, but her tissue type was difficult to match. Believe me. Everything that could have been done was done."

"Why didn't she talk to us about it? Tell us?" Jade asks.

"She never wanted you to worry about her. All she ever thought about was you girls. She wanted to protect you."

"Was she in the hospital?" I ask.

"Yes."

"That's why all the hospital bills," Jade says to me.

"What hospital bills?" my dad asks.

"They're at Grandmom's house. I saw three of them and they're really expensive. There's no way Grandmom can pay them."

"The bills should have never gone to your grandmother."

"Kenisha and I are selling some of the furniture from before. I already checked with a few consignment shops and showed them photos. They're very interested. But it won't be enough."

"I'm gonna be making good money from dancing," I say.

"There's no way working at Freeman can make a dent in what we have to pay," Jade says.

My dad smiles. "No, your paycheck is yours, Kenisha."

"That's not what I mean," I say, and then all of a sudden the office door opens and Courtney comes in. She has Jr. and Jason by the hand and the baby in the carrier. She stands in the center of the room glaring at my dad. "Y'all go ahead to your father. He's taking care of you tonight."

"Not now, Courtney," my dad says.

"Can we watch television again?" Jr. asks his mom.

"Go to your dad. Mom's going out with her friends—the ones he hasn't already slept with."

"You don't know what the hell you're talking about and you need to chill on that bullshit in front of my kids."

"What are you talking about? I know for a fact you slept with Yolanda, Angel, Brandy, Olivia and Monique. They told me."

"They lie. I don't even know those women."

"Can we watch television again, please?" Jr. asks again.

"Well, they know you," she insists.

"You need to stay here with the kids because I'll be leaving in a few. I need to go to work tonight," my dad says.

"Oh, hell, no. You don't work on Sundays," Courtney responds quickly.

"I make the money in this house every day."

"Uh-uh, no, not this time. It's my turn. I'm going out this time. I'm sick and tired of you leaving me here with the kids while you hang out all night with your whores and skanks."

That's when the argument really begins. She starts yelling and he starts yelling.

"Can we watch television again, please?" Jr. asks again.

"Please," Jason adds.

"Sure, go ahead," I say. They immediately run out of the office.

So apparently that's the end of the conversation. Jade and I don't stay long after that. The baby's asleep and we take the boys into the family room to watch their television show. The argument calms down to rolling eyes and mean looks. Jade and I leave.

We talk about what my dad told us just about all the way home. I even look the word up on Google with my cell phone while she drives. Again we lapse into silence. As we get closer to the house Jade chuckles. I look over at her. She laughs.

"What's funny," I ask.

"Oh, my God, seriously, do they do that a lot?" Jade asks.

I get it. "Oh, hell, yeah, all the time," I say.

"They need some serious anger management counseling."

I shake my head. "They need a lot more than that."

We keep laughing as she drives. Then Jade all of a sudden changes the subject when she stops at a traffic light. "So what you said back there in your dad's office—what did you mean about making good money?"

"Nothing," I lie evasively.

"Come on, tell me."

"It was nothing."

"Kenisha, I can see it in your face. Something's going on. Tell me. What is it?" The light changes, but she's still looking at me. The driver behind her hits his horn and she drives off.

"Nothing," I repeat.

"You might as well tell me 'cause you know I'm gonna find out. And if you're doing what I think you are, then you need to stop it now."

Jade does this psychology thing on people sometimes. It's the same thing our mom used to do before I figured it out. See, she says this open statement and this is the part where you start wondering if she already knows what's going on. Then you start talking and tell her everything. But I know that game and I'm not playing. She's right. She'll find out what's up, but only after I have the money in my hand.

Since I don't respond how she wants she drops the subject, then pulls up in front of the house. "Kenisha, I can't stop you from doing what you're doing. I can only warn you."

"What do you mean? Warn me about what?"

"You asked me before about what happened between Tyrece and Taj and about getting the money from him to pay the hospital bills, remember?"

"Yeah, I remember," I say.

"The reason is that he doesn't have the money."

"What? But he's rich."

"Very few people know this, but Ty's broke. He sank everything he had into his production company. Now it's gone."

"How? What happened?"

"Taj was underage when he signed her. After her first CD she got a better offer from another company and wanted to take it, but she was tied to Ty's company for seven more years. To get out of the contract she threatened Ty with a sexual assault and statutory rape charge. He let her out. Taj left the company and it went bankrupt. What's left the IRS is taking."

"I didn't know. I'm sorry."

"He's okay. He's working hard to get back on top. But know that Taj can't be trusted. She's too focused on getting to the top any way she can and if that means screwing people, she will."

"Jade, I got this," I say assuredly.

She nods. "Okay, if you say so."

I nod. "I'll talk to you later." I get out of the car and hurry in the house as she drives off back to school. I reset the alarm, grab some water and a sandwich, 'cause I'm starved after dinner at my dad's, then head upstairs. My grandmother is home, but she's asleep in her chair with the television on. I don't want to disturb her, so I just go up to my room.

I chill and lay low the rest of the weekend. I keep thinking about what my dad told us. My mom was in so much pain and never said a word to us. I feel so bad now. My grandmother wants to talk, but I can't. I still need to understand, so she lets me have my space.

Jalisa and Diamond call, but I don't say much. Terrence calls, but I don't pick up. I don't feel like being bothered right now. I need to do what I need to do. Nobody understands, so I just do me.

Monday morning everything is back to normal or just about. It's spring break, so I get to chill all week. I don't go on my run because it's raining hard outside. It's the perfect day to stay in bed late, so I do. I know my grandmother is at her volunteer job and Jade's at school, so I have the whole house to myself. I grab something to eat around noon, then go back up to my bedroom and chill some more.

I do the same thing the next two days. But on Wednesday afternoon everything changes. I get a text message from Taj. She's back in town. She wants to do a rehearsal tomorrow since the video shoot has been moved up to this weekend. Okay, that's perfect for me 'cause I had no idea how I was gonna skip out on school for two days next week. She also mentions more changes and she has a surprise for me. This ought to be good.

twenty

All Alone Between a Rock and a Hard Place

LiveJournal Homepage Spotlight: May 10, 2012
kenishi_wa K Lewis
Fate has a way of jumping up and pushing you down when you least expect it. Well, here it is again.
Link * Add to Memories * Share

It's Thursday morning. I get up early because I'm excited. I really wish my girls could be with me for this, but I'll tell them everything as soon as it's over. I know they'll be happy for me once they know why I'm doing this. So I shower, get dressed, grab my dance bag and then head down the back stairs to the kitchen. I want to get to the studio early to maybe run through the routine before everyone gets there. I grab a bottle of water and leave a note on the refrigerator door about studying at the library all day.

Since it rained the past few days, it's good to see the sun is finally out. Maybe it's a good sign. I leave the house right after rush hour, so traffic has died down and there's barely anyone on the streets. I get to the studio as I planned, early. There's craziness going on outside with people everywhere. I walk in the door and see everything is different. There's a notice that we're on the first level today. I follow the signs to a large open space that looks more like a warehouse than a dance studio.

As soon as I walk in I see this huge green screen up along the back of one wall and the floor is padded with soft tiles in the same green color. There are props everywhere. A fake bedroom set is on one side and an outdoor gazebo scene is on the other. There's a lot of activity. People are everywhere—setting up cameras, moving things around and changing lighting. I see Linda and Pamela sitting off to the side talking. They still have on their regular street clothes. I go over to them. "Hey, what's up? What's with all the people and cameras outside?"

"Taj has an interview on one of the music cable shows so she wants this to be a dress rehearsal."

Shit. "A dress rehearsal—but I forgot to bring the bag."

"Doesn't matter, they've changed the costume again."

"Thank God," I say, obviously relieved.

"Not so fast. It could be worse, if that's even possible," Pam says, chuckling.

"What could be worse than that hot mess?" I ask.

"I guess we'll see in a little bit," Linda adds.

"What's with the video camera in here, too? Are they filming us today also?"

"Nah, Taj is trying to sell a reality show to television."

"A reality show about what? Her?" I ask.

Linda and Pamela laugh. "Kenisha, haven't you caught on yet? Whatever it is, it's always about Taj."

I sit down with them and just watch the craziness unfold. I see that there are a lot more people here now, including a guy who is absolutely gorgeous. "Wow, who's he?"

"He's the model for the video shoot."

I look around. "Where are Donna and Connie?"

"They quit," Linda says.

"They what?" I say, surprised to hear this. "Why?"

"Are you kidding? Do you even have to ask? This is the worst job in the business. Who can really blame them for quitting?" Linda says.

"What are they gonna do now?"

"I spoke with them last night," Pam says. "They both got new jobs, so it's all good."

A few minutes later Money Train comes in. He looks around, then sees us sitting here. He smiles and nods, but mainly at Linda. She gets up and goes over to him. Anybody can see that there's more than just a passing friendship between them. I look at Pam. "What's the…"

Pam just shakes her head. "Don't even say it."

I don't. I watch as she pulls him close and whispers something into his ear. He's smiling. After a while they walk away. I just shake my head. A few minutes after that Taj comes in from the front door with her usual entourage. But this time she has a plus one—Terrence is with her. I swear my jaw drops to the floor.

He just walks in like it's no big deal. I watch, speechless, as he looks around the huge area casually and then he sees me. He's stunned at first and then he smiles and gets ready to come over to me. Taj grabs his arms and holds tight. Then he removes her hand and comes to me. "Hey," he says, smiling that smile that always gets to me.

"Hey," I say nonchalantly. Pam gets up to find Linda.

"I've been calling you," Terrence says.

"Yeah, I know" is all I say, without offering any more of an explanation for not getting back to him. There's one thing that's certain about Terrence—he's no fool. He knows I'm pissed, he knows why and he knows he's wrong.

"So what are you doing here?"

"I'm working," I say. "What about you? What are you doing here?" Just as I say the words, I see Taj hurrying over to us.

"Hey, I guess you see my surprise," Taj says as she grabs Terrence's arm and holds on to him just like I did the first time we met after the party that night. But then I was holding my lawnmower guy's arm, not her. So now I'm just looking at her holding him. My thoughts go in a million different directions—none of them good.

"Taj told me she had a special surprise on the set of her video and that I should come down and check it out," he says, answering the question I almost forgot I even asked.

I look at Taj. She's wearing a thick terry robe and stilettos and her makeup is already done. Her hair is weaved blond and long all the way down her back, then teased out in big wild waves. She's just standing there smiling at me. But it's more than just a smile. It's that catty shit I know all too well. Then she tilts her head. "Surprise."

"Are you staying for the whole thing?" I ask him, ignoring her.

"Nah, I'm going to class this afternoon."

"Aw," Taj says, poking her lower lip out babyishly.

I know his class schedule. He has a communications lecture this afternoon. We start talking about the assignment he has to turn in today. It's one I helped him with. So we're laughing about the assignment and Taj is looking completely left out. She's just standing there looking stupid.

"Well, maybe *I* can convince you to skip class and stay with me."

"Nah, school trumps videos."

"Are you sure I can't tempt you?" Taj says as she starts

rubbing his chest. He stops her and moves her hand away and looks at me. I just shake my head.

Okay, I am too pissed. I just look at her. She did all this shit on purpose—why, I have no idea. If she thinks she's getting my lawnmower guy, she's wrong. Just then Magic Man comes over to us, clapping his hands to get our attention.

"Okay, okay, we're on the clock, people. Let's do this. You have thirty minutes to change into the costumes and stretch. Let's go."

I look at Terrence. "I gotta get ready to…"

"Go, yes. Don't worry. He's fine. I'll take good care of him," Taj says, rubbing her chest against his arm on purpose.

I just turn and leave. Pam walks up beside me as I head to one of the dressing rooms in the back. We each have a small cubby to put our things and to change. She holds up the hanger with her costume. "Check it out, not too bad," she says.

I hold mine up, too. It's a pair of white skintight dance pants with a matching tank top and white army boots. There's also a midriff white fur jacket. "Oh, my God, this is so much better than that other outfit. Thank God," I say again.

"For real." She obviously agrees. "Hey, who was that guy with Taj?" she asks. "Do you know him?"

"Believe it or not, that was my boyfriend," I say.

"Golden rule, Kenisha—never bring your man to within twenty miles of Taj."

"I didn't bring him. She did."

"Damn," Pam says, "that's a new low even for her. I swear she's like a man vacuum. She literally sucks them in, and I don't mean that figuratively. And if they're not interested in her on their own, she goes after them full force until they are. I learned that lesson the hard way."

"The hard way? What do you mean?" I say, changing into my sweats and tank top.

"Taj went after my boyfriend about a year ago. After she got him to prove that she could, she dumped him."

"Damn, just like that."

"Yep, just like that. I think it's the attention. It's some kind of ego boost. I'm sure Sigmund Freud would love a conversation with her," Pam says, bending and stretching her legs out.

I think about my psychologist, Dr. Tubbs. I can just see him trying to figure her crazy ass out. "Did you take him back?" I ask, getting down on the floor to start stretching, too.

"Oh, hell, no, his shit is old. I figured that if he's weak enough to follow after someone like her, he doesn't deserve someone like me. Besides, I'm seeing someone so much better."

"But I don't get it. She did that to you and you're still here dancing with her. Why?"

"Money," she says, "this job pays good money and I need it. College classes aren't cheap. I put up with her bullshit for one reason—to make the money."

"You're not the only one. Money's the only reason I'm here, too."

Fifteen minutes later Linda joins us. We've stretched and are getting ready to do a quick run-through. Taj, still in her robe, is sitting with her entourage and the reality show film crew, talking. I look around for Terrence, expecting to see him somewhere around her, but he's not. He's over talking to the guy setting up the music. I look back at Taj—she's watching Terrence, too.

Devon, Magic Man and the director call us over to see the video storyboards. Our part is basically dancing our routine with Taj in front of us. Then it ends with Taj lying on a fur rug holding on to the male model. The song is called *I Got Him Now*. The basic idea is that we're his past lovers and she has him now.

Afterward, Magic Man walks us through the moves to make sure the timing is right. Then he talks to Taj about her part. She's all smiles and laughter for the reality show camera, acting like she actually knows what she's doing.

"All right, let's try this," the director says. I put on my fur jacket. Pam puts on her tuxedo jacket and Linda puts on her military jacket. Taj takes off her robe. She's dressed in a skin-colored too-skimpy bra top with matching too-tight boy's briefs and six-inch stiletto thigh-high boots. She gets in place in front of us. The music starts. She begins lip-syncing the song. She's doing her dance steps awkwardly as we dance our routine. The model is in place and she's making everything look awkward. She stops suddenly and complains that the set is too noisy.

The director makes just about everyone leave, except Taj's entourage and the reality show film crew. We try the routine once more. This time we get all the way through, ending with her and the model on the fur-topped bed. Now she complains that we're not doing the right steps and we're throwing her off. We try it again. Halfway through we stop.

"This is all bullshit!" Taj yells. Everybody looks at her. "This is my video and I know what I want and how I want it and this isn't it." She goes over to the director, Magic Man and Devon.

"Taj, this is exactly what we talked about," Magic Man says. "We've been practicing this routine for the past two weeks. What's wrong with it?"

"I want it different, sexier." She pouts. "Get rid of him. He's all wrong. There's no chemistry. There's no way anyone is gonna believe he's my man. He's pathetic."

"Excuse me," the guy says, "I'm a top-paid model. I don't need this diva drama and her attitude." He walks away.

"All right, wait, hold up. Everybody just calm down. We can make this work. Taj, trust me, the two of you look perfect up there."

"No, I'm not feeling it," she insists. "I need somebody real—somebody that stands out. Someone my fans can relate to and connect with."

"What are you talking about?" Devon says.

She stops a minute and then looks around at all of us. "Just get rid of him. I have a better idea."

They call the model back over. A few seconds later he starts cussing, then grabs his stuff and storms out.

"What's all that about?" I ask quietly.

"What else? More Taj drama," Linda says.

"Looks like she fired the model," Pamela says.

"So now how is she supposed to…" I begin, but don't have to finish. I know exactly what she's gonna do.

"Terrence, can you come over here?" she purrs.

One of the guys at the mix table hits Terrence's arm. He removes the headphones and looks up at me. Taj calls him over to her again. He goes over. They speak a moment with Devon and the director. I can't hear what they're saying, but I know exactly what's going on. Taj got rid of the model to use Terrence in the love scene. They're nodding their heads as Taj talks. Terrence shakes his head no, then walks away.

I'm standing to the side and he comes right to me. "I gotta get to class. I'll call you later," he says. I nod and smile. He kisses me and leaves. I can see Taj is furious.

twenty-one

Blindsided by BS

kenishi_wa K Lewis
*I wonder why I'm doing this. Then all of the sudden
I know—'cause nobody else will. At some point you
have to stand up to the stupidity.*
10 May * Like * Comment * Share

WE start dancing again and I'm kicking my ass working
hard. It's more and more apparent that Taj can't keep up.
The other people here know, the director knows and she
sure as hell knows. So we keep going, hitting every movement exactly as Magic Man wants. Taj, on the other hand,
keeps making us stop and complaining about how we're
too close to her and she feels crowded and we're cramping
her style and messing her up. At one point she stops and
just screams. We all stop instantly and just stand looking at
her crazy ass.

Two of her entourage go to her with a towel and water.
She talks to them as we stand there wiping sweat from our
faces. She looks in the mirror and scowls. "What the hell
are you doing behind me," she yells. Her reality film crew
steps up and starts filming again.

We all look around to see who she's talking to. Then I

realize she's yelling at me. "Yeah, you, what's wrong with you? What's your problem? Can't you take directions? Obviously I made a mistake in trying to give your snot ass a chance and get your poor no-class ass out of the ghetto. Can't you see that you're screwing us up?"

My jaw drops. I can't believe she's gonna stand there and call me out for her stiff no-dancing ass. "I'm doing the routine Magic Man showed me," I defend myself.

"Are you saying I'm wrong, that I don't know what I'm doing?"

Duh, it's obvious that she can't dance and she's an idiot, too. But I know I can't say that, so I just smile 'cause I need the money. "I'm saying that I'm doing what I'm supposed to."

She's really going off now, screaming and moving closer and closer to me. Her entourage steps up to back her. "What, you can't hear me? I'm talking to you. This is supposed to make me look good, to highlight me. Don't you get it? I'm the star here. I'm the one people pay money to see, not your no-dancing ass. It's all about me."

"Like I said, I'm doing the steps and routine Magic Man taught us, then changed so you can keep up," I say.

I can see the fury blaze in her eyes. I don't exactly call her out for being the one that keeps screwing up, but I definitely make it plain that she needs to look at her own shit. So all of a sudden she comes toward me and nearly trips on her high heels. One of her girls grabs her arm to prevent her from falling. She quickly shakes her off like she's being held back. It's so stupid it's comical. A couple of the other people snicker and she glares at them, but keeps her anger focused on me.

Now she's really screaming all up in my face, telling me

how I can't dance and how she was wrong to include me. Oh, my God, I swear she smells like pure alcohol. No wonder she's messing up. She's drunk.

I don't move, but I swear nothing is worth this heffer screaming at me. I ball up my fist like my mom taught me and I'm just about to knock the shit out of her when all of a sudden Pamela comes over and pulls my arms away. "We got this, Taj," she says.

"Yeah, you'd better handle your girl and teach her how things work around here. Nobody makes me look bad."

It's on the tip of my tongue to tell her that nobody has to make her look bad, she's looking bad all by herself, but Linda steps up, blocking us. They pull me away and start talking. At this point I'm really not hearing it. I'm too pissed. I can feel the tears welling up in my eyes. I know I can dance and I know I'm doing everything the other dancers are doing. It's not me.

Now she's completely surrounded by her entourage. They're trying to calm her down. "Don't be all up in my face, Devon, you need to talk to Magic Man and the rest of those skanky dancers. Better yet, get rid of all of them. I don't need them. I'm the star. I'm the only one here who knows what's up. They can't even dance—none of them."

Magic Man steps up and pulls Taj and her whole crew off to the side. Now we're just standing around and all you can hear is her screaming and yelling about getting no respect and how she wants more money and how she's the next Beyoncé and everybody around her are jealous assholes.

The director comes over to us. "Look, Taj is under some stress. You're all doing a great job. We're gonna order some Chinese food. What do you want?"

By now we've been here all morning and afternoon. I'm

starved, but there's no way I want anything from Taj. So he keeps going on that Taj needs to eat something and she's a little irritable. Is he joking? She's a friggin' lunatic. I've never seen anybody go mental like that, not even Court-ney, and she the craziest person I know.

"I'm done here." I head to the dressing room to get my stuff. Pamela and Linda follow, trying to get me to calm down. Magic Man stops me and asks me to stay. "No, I don't need this."

"Where do you think you're going?" Taj says, following me.

"As far away from your crazy ass as possible," I say, get-ting my stuff from the cubby.

"Bullshit. You need to get back here. I own you. You signed a contract," she says, playing to the camera still film-ing her.

I start laughing and open my dance bag. I pull out the large white envelope Devon gave me. I never signed it. I toss it at her. "You mean this contract? The one I never signed?"

"It doesn't matter. I still own your ass, bitch. You want to get paid—you gotta go through me."

Fine, I've been called that before. No big deal. "Yeah, right, whatever," I say, and keep walking out.

When we get back to the main open area she pushes me in the back. I stumble forward, but keep my balance. I turn around just as she goes to push me again. I move to the side. She stumbles and I push her away from me and keep going. She grabs my arm and pulls me. "You ain't going nowhere until I say so." Bad idea, 'cause I turn around swinging. I barely clip her chin and she looks at me like I lost my mind. "What the hell is wrong with you, bitch? You hit me."

"Then keep your hands off me," I warn. I turn around to keep walking out. Everybody else is just staring, shocked at what's happening. I hear her coming up behind me again. She's yelling and calling me names. She pushes me once more. This time I fall to my hands and knees. For real, all bets are off now. She's standing over me with her crew behind her. I have no idea what she's thinking. I guess maybe she lost her mind or something because her stupid entourage is here to back her up. But at this point I really don't care if I get jumped as long as I kick her ass first.

So she's still talking bad. "Yeah, that's right. I pushed your ass down. What you gonna do about it, bitch?" I stand up and she steps in my face and goes to push me again. As soon as she reaches her hands out I block her and slap her across her face just like my mom taught me. It was hard, solid and perfect. My hand stings, so I know her face must be on fire. Her jaw drops and she grabs the side of her face and screams.

The loud pop of my smack makes everybody gasp and cringe. I guess they didn't think anybody would step up to the little bullying tyrant. Seriously, I wasn't playing. I'd had enough of Taj and her stupid drama calling me out.

"Bitch," she screams again.

I'm not walking away this time. I stand there waiting. If she wants to start something again I will seriously finish it. Pamela and Linda come to stand beside me. Devon and Magic Man try to calm Taj down again, but she's over-the-top ballistic now. Her blond weave is all over her head and her makeup is smeared and just sad.

I start smiling, then laughing. All I can think of is my fight with Regan at Hazelhurst and how they still talk about me yanking her weave out. All of a sudden Pam and Linda start laughing, too. I guess they think I'm laughing because Taj looks like a complete fool. Well, I guess I'm laughing about that, too.

"So y'all stupid asses laughing and gonna take her side."

"Taj, why do you have to do this drama every time? Just shut up and chill out," Pamela says. Then one of Taj's girls steps up to Pamela and gets all in her face. "You need to back your girl out of my face right now."

"Or what?" the girl, says bumping into Pam.

"You'd better back the hell up," she warns again.

I'm looking at Pamela and she's not playing. It looks like she's about to go off on the girl. She gets bumped again. Then she does. She swings and connects with the girl's right eye. She goes down like a rock. One of the guys in Taj's entourage jumps up in Linda's face. She kicks him dead center, still wearing the hard army boots from the video shoot. He doubles over, holding his groin while screaming and cussing. The whole place is about to erupt.

Taj's eyes widen to dinner plates. "Somebody call the police. I want to file assault charges on these bitches. Y'all saw what they did."

Okay, now I know I gotta get out of here for real.

"Do you really think you're gonna ever work in this business again, ever? I'm gonna make sure none of my friends hire you to dance."

"You don't have any friends," Pam says.

"You got that right," Linda adds.

"Yo, what up? What's going on in here?" Everybody turns around. Money Train walks in, seeing us all gathered in the center of the room.

Taj starts yelling again about how we attacked her and her friends. "Yeah, bitches, that's right. I got friends—deep-pocket friends—so don't even think your asses are getting paid."

I turn around to leave, then she starts getting personal. "So what you gonna do now, Kenisha? I know you need the money," she taunts.

"Back off," Money Train says.

"Kenisha."

I turn around and see Terrence looking around for me. He pushes a couple of people out of the way and comes over to me.

"Go, and take your bitch-ass boy with you. I don't need you and I don't need him. You just like you was before, T, a punk-ass. I give you the opportunity of a lifetime to work with me and you turn me down for her. Fine, keep him. I got my man and he's gonna kick his ass," she says.

Money Train just looks at her and shakes his head. "Girl, this shit's done. A'ight, listen up—if y'all want to get paid, y'all need to get the hell up out of here now."

It was like someone yelled fire 'cause people started moving like the building was about to collapse. Devon, Magic Man, the film crew, were the first to leave. In, like, two minutes the place was cleared out. So we're all just standing there again and now all I can think about is how Terrence was fighting before and lost a scholarship and almost had to quit college. I can't let that happen again.

"Come on, let's go," I say, taking his hand. We start leaving.

"Go, bitch-asses," Taj yells. Pamela and Linda turn to follow. "Yeah, y'all leave, too, 'cause y'all ain't never working as dancers again. You won't even be able to strip when I'm done with you."

"Yeah, whatever," Linda says.

"Where you think you're going?" Taj asks.

I turn around and see Money Train is leaving with us—or more specifically, with Linda. He doesn't answer. I look at Taj. Her mouth is wide open in shock. It's obvious Money Train just took his side and it's not hers.

So we get outside and we all just start laughing. It's not that anything is funny. It's just that we're all kinda shocked by what just happened. Money Train introduces himself to Terrence and they start talking. Linda goes up and stands by his side. "Come on, let's get out of here," Money Train says, then turns to the shiny silver 2011 Maybach Guard parked directly in front of the studio.

We all climb in. I can't believe his car. It's gorgeous. It's huge inside and I've never seen anything like it.

"Where to?" Money Train asks.

I give him my address and he drives off. Everybody's talking and laughing and I'm just sitting here still in shock. So much for earning money dancing. I look down at the costume I never changed out of. Maybe I can sell the fake-fur jacket.

About fifteen minutes later the car pulls up in front of my house. I see Jade and Tyrece standing outside talking. Linda, Pamela and Money Train want to meet Tyrece, so everybody gets out of the car. I look up and see my grandmother sitting on the front porch with her two friends, Ms. Edith and Ms. Grace. I just shake my head and get out last. I know I have a lot of explaining to do.

We all start talking at once, explaining what just happened. Pamela basically takes the lead in telling the story and it comes out more funny and zany than anything. So there's a lot of laughter and jokes. Except I know my grandmother isn't really laughing. I know I need to tell her the for-real story.

Tyrece, Money Train, Terrence, Jade, Linda and Pamela stay outside talking. I go inside and sit in the kitchen with my grandmother. I know she's waiting for me to say something. Even though she already knows what happened today she doesn't really know why. I take a deep breath and shake my head. I'm not even sure where to start. So I just jump right in. "Today was a mess and I know I made it. I should never have lied and try to do this by myself and without telling anyone. I know I disappointed you."

"Why'd you do it?"

"I was trying to get money to help."

"Money to help with what?" my grandmother asks.

"The hospital bills," I say.

"What?"

Jade walks into the kitchen. "Grandmom, we know about the hospital bills. Kenisha saw them. It's a lot of money and you can't pay something like that by yourself. We're not gonna let you sacrifice the house. We want to help."

"Oh, babies…" she begins slowly.

"Jade and I talked when you were in Georgia," I say. "We're selling some of the furniture from the Virginia house to help raise money, but I knew it wasn't gonna be a lot so that's when I agreed to dance in the video with Taj. Jade, you were right—she's not gonna pay me."

"That's Taj," she says, shaking her head.

"I worked so hard just to wind up with nothing."

"You didn't wind up with nothing. You tried to do something good and that's always worth something. Now, do me a favor, both of you—let me take care of paying the hospital bills."

We nod slowly.

"Now, who's hungry?"

"I'm starved," I say.

My grandmother cooks dinner while I tell her and Jade about the fight with Taj. Jade can't stop laughing, and although my grandmother tries not to, she still chuckles and enjoys the stories. After dinner I go up to my room and hit up Jalisa and Diamond. We're all on the phone and I'm telling them about what I was really doing and what happened today. At first they're upset because I didn't tell them before and then they're okay. After I tell them about the fight they're laughing hysterically. We hang up two hours later.

I can't sleep so I grab my recipe book. Everything seems to begin and end with it. I open it to the last notation. It's all about my download drama. The video went viral for a minute and just that quickly it was replaced with kittens playing in a box. So much for being a cyber celeb.

twenty-two

Still in Control-ish

kenishi_wa K Lewis
They always talk about finding your path. Well, what about if the path divides? Do you go right or do you go left or do you just stand still and wait for another path to come along? If there's one thing I know—there's always another path.
11 May * Like * Comment * Share

I wake up at four-thirty in the morning with tears in my eyes. For the first time in a long time they're not for my mother. I dreamed about her but right now I'm crying for me. I stare up at the ceiling, thinking about everything that's happened in the past few days. It seems like whatever I do it all comes back to the same thing. As a daughter I could have done better, been better, but it's too late now.

I get up and take my usual seat at the window. It's too dark to see anything outside, but I do see a blue glow next door, second floor. It's Terrence's bedroom window. He's either watching television or playing a video game. I grab my cell off the charger and call him. He picks up on the third ring. "Yeah."

"Hey, you up?" I ask.

"I am now. What's going on?" he says sleepily.

"I can't sleep."

"What's wrong—bad dreams?"

"No, actually," I say, "good dreams."

He pauses for a moment. "Want to run?"

"Nah."

"Want to talk?" he asks.

"Yeah, meet me outside."

"Okay. Ten minutes."

I put on some sweatpants and a T-shirt, then tiptoe downstairs to the kitchen and turn the light on. I turn off the alarm and open the back door. Terrence is already sitting on the back steps waiting for me. He's wearing a T-shirt and jeans and turns when I open the door. As soon as I sit down beside him he puts his arm around me and pulls me close. I rest my head on his shoulder and I'm immediately comforted. I take a deep breath and slowly exhale.

We don't say anything right away. We just sit listening to the night sounds and feeling the cool breeze around us. This is what I love about hanging with my lawnmower guy. He knows just what I need when I need it. "How'd it go?" he asks.

I know exactly what he's talking about—my conversation with my grandmother and Jade. "It was okay. I'm glad we talked. I think we all needed it, and they enjoyed my Taj stories."

He chuckles.

All of the sudden tears start welling in my eyes. I can't stop them. "I still can't believe that I went through all that drama with Taj and I'm not even gonna get paid."

"Actually, I think you are." He pulls an envelope out of

his pocket. "This is for you. Money Train gave it to me last night."

I open the envelope and tears start flowing. It's a check for three thousand dollars plus a five hundred bonus. "Are you kidding me?"

"What is it?" Terrence asks.

I give him the check. He smiles and nods. "Now that's what I'm talking about."

I hug him and kiss him and hug him some more. I can't stop laughing and clapping my hands. This is the best ever. "I can't believe he did this."

"He's a pretty good guy. He told me to give him a call this summer. He's got a scholarship and a job waiting for me."

"For real? That's great!"

"What is all this noise out here? Do you realize it's after five o'clock in the morning and good people are still trying to get some sleep?"

"Sorry. Good morning, Grandmom."

"Good morning, Mrs. King," Terrence says.

"Good morning. Now since you're already up, anybody want some breakfast?"

"Oh, yeah, pancakes and sausage," Terrence suggests.

"How about some grit, bacon and hash browns, too."

He slaps his hands together. "Sounds good to me."

"Grandmom, look. I got paid for dancing." I stand up and show her the check excitedly.

"That's wonderful."

"I'll sign it and you can give it to the hospital."

She shakes her head. "No, that's your money. The hospital bill is paid."

"What? How? Who paid it?" I question.

"Your father did."

"Dad paid it," I say, unbelieving.

"I spoke with him last night after you went up to your room. We talked. I guess it was a long time coming," she says, then pauses a few seconds. "By the way, you're gonna have to tell him about your little escapade the past few weeks. I don't think he's going to be too happy. Consequences."

I nod. "I know. I'll call him after breakfast."

"Good," she says, then goes back inside to start cooking.

Terrence and I return to sitting on the back step. We're talking and laughing about the drama with Taj, then I hear a beep.

"Is that your phone?"

"Yeah, it's a missed text message," I say, pulling my cell out of my pants pocket. "It's probably Jalisa or Diamond." I look at the text and then start laughing. "Oh, my God, you're not gonna believe this."

"What, who is it?"

"It's Taj."

He starts laughing, too. "Let me guess, she wants her costume back."

"Nope."

"Good, 'cause I kinda like you in all that white," he says, licking his lips and pulling me close.

I laugh and push away. I know he's joking. "You're never gonna believe this. She says that the reality show people saw what she sent them. They like it. They want her to do a pilot."

"Just what we need—another stupid reality show on TV."

"But wait, that's not the best part. They want me to be

in it, too. It seems Taj and I have good opposing energy."
I can barely say the words without laughing.

"Are you kidding me?"

"No, that's what she says, see?" I give him my cell phone
and he reads the message.

"You gonna do it?" he asks, giving me the phone back.

"Nah, this right here is reality enough for me."

"Yeah, me, too," he says.

"Come on, let's go eat. We have the whole day ahead of
us and you never know what kind of drama is gonna happen next."

★ ★ ★ ★ ★

KPAA993081ITR

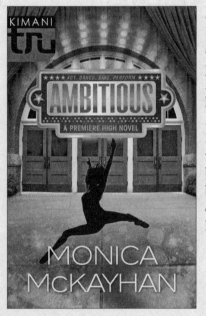